Operation Gunfleet

Also by Robert Wallace

The Valentine Series

Valentines Cup

Crimson Wing

Monkeypuzzle

Other novels

One Single Ticket

A Victorian detective thriller based on
real events and revolutionary ideas
from Isambard Kingdom Brunel

Fables and Folk

A collection of West Country supernatural short stories

The Betrayal of Jacqueline Flower

A psychological crime thriller with a twisting storyline

About the Author

Robert Wallace was born and raised in Bristol and spent many years working in the medical field which took him to Europe, the United States, Japan, Australia and Scandinavia. It sparked a lifelong interest in travel. His work involves turning historical events into works of semi-fiction, retaining the factual background, creating fictional characters to share their lives with real people.

ROBERT WALLACE

OPERATION GUNFLEET

THE FINAL STORY IN THE VALENTINE SERIES

TradShack

Operation Gunfleet is a work of fiction. Any resemblance to actual events or persons, living or dead, is entirely coincidental.

Cover design by www. tradshack.com

Published by www. tradshack.com

ISBN: 979-8-8528759-5-2

"And ye shall know the truth and the truth shall make you free."

Book of JOHN V111 – XXX11

Allen Dulles, the fifth and longest-serving director of the Central Intelligence Agency (CIA) had this biblical quotation carved in stone in the lobby of their HQ at Langley, Virginia, USA.

Jessica

Post-war London
a year after the German surrender

Waterloo Station, England

IF I'D KNOWN I WAS GOING TO DIE THAT DAY, I might have done things differently. At least I'd have been more cautious. But there we are. I'd known I was being followed from the moment I left Lyons' Cornerhouse on Shaftesbury Avenue. It was obvious. I don't know why exactly, a presence, a shadow, a feeling. Call it instinct if you like. I had been taught fieldcraft while working in Washington as a courier for the US Department of Defense. There were telltale signs. First and most importantly, you had to double-check; to assume you were being pursued and then make sure they didn't cotton on ...

But this man was good; in fact, I'd soon realise there were two of them. I walked towards Victoria Embankment in the direction of Charing Cross Station and quickened my pace. I had a reasonable walk ahead of me to my tiny bedsit on Blackfriars Road. It was getting dark and there was a damp, misty chill drifting off the Thames. Today had been my third meeting with Professor Nicholas Brimblecombe, eminent chief of British Intelligence.

"You're looking well, Miss Hope," he had said wryly as I sat down opposite him at a table in the tea house, "considering the risk you are taking."

"And so are you, professor," I replied with equal formality. "We are both taking a risk, given the rather unusual circumstances."

"That is true, I suppose." He paused. "Ah, I see you have something for me, judging by the package under your arm?" He pursed his lips the way he did and raised his eyebrows.

"No," I said smiling. "Just some shopping." We both knew that wasn't true, of course. I was here for a very specific reason.

"Very flat looking shopping, I must say." He pointed with his eyes, a hint of a smile.

We had a similar sense of humour, and I could understand why and how he had risen to occupy such an important position. He was a dapper fellow, not dissimilar in appearance to film director Alfred Hitchcock: very well-attired, eloquently spoken and not given to small talk. We had gone over again exactly what I had seen outside the huts at Bletchley Park where I'd worked. Who were these people? Did they speak to one another? What did they say? Endless questions. He was pedantic to the point of irritation, but then, I suppose he had to be.

But the most important thing on the agenda today was the documents he had asked me to bring to substantiate my story: the package under my arm he had so correctly observed. He wanted evidence because what I was alleging was a serious breach of security. And the claim was now here on the table in front of us. He went through each document carefully, and initially without comment.

Firstly: A US Pentagon Stores Requisition Memo. It detailed a formal request that British Comms Equipment should be released into the care of one Captain Larry Boseman, US 6813th Detachment. The memo was dated August 1945 and signed off by Colonel Beckworth. There were another couple of signatories whose names were illegible, but their ranks were not.

The second was a typed memorandum from me to the masterminds at Bletchley Park: Dilly Knox, Alan Turing and so on. There was a carbon copy addressed to Captain Jerry Roberts, who worked on the pioneering Tunny codebreaking op. My memo explained my fears that 6813th were surely NOT authorised to sanction Comms equipment on the apparent whim of one American Colonel. I had attached a copy of the SR Memo, but never sent it because I was frightened.

Thirdly, and on a highly personal level, a letter from John Beckworth to me stating that our love affair was over. He had enclosed $200 and said (very nicely dressed up, I have to say) that any secrets I may have overheard, or read, if made public could be the subject of a Military Tribunal. He was referring of course to the Memo, which he had seen me photograph. Beckworth was threatening me.

Once our business at Lyons' Cornerhouse was concluded, Brim's instructions were clear: he would retain the documents and I was to return to my flat and pack not only my belongings but also anything that might further implicate Beckworth, no matter how trivial. He would then send a car and re-locate me immediately to safe haven out of reach of the US Army. In particular Beckworth or any of his associates.

*

I climbed the steps of Hungerford Footbridge and headed across the river towards Waterloo Station. It was five-thirty in the evening; I could see Charing Cross Station was busy with commuters as I walked away. I turned. There he was again, similar to Eliot Ness: the collar of his raincoat was turned up, cigarette in the corner of his mouth, newspaper under his arm.

"Sorry, love." A muscular young man suddenly collided into me with such force it knocked the wind out of me. It was even busier now, five forty-five, as I descended the steps at the other end of the footbridge. My ribcage felt so agonisingly painful that it hurt to breathe. I wondered if the man had broken a couple of my ribs and jagged edges were poking into my lung. Dammit, I realised the thug had stolen my shoulder bag by distracting me. My house keys and purse were in it. And my Driving Licence.

I was outside the back of Waterloo Station now, a quiet spot by the river, gasping for air and clutching my chest in sheer agony. How on earth would I get into my building? It was sure to be empty at this hour. I started to panic. Suddenly Eliot Ness was beside me and another man behind. I was confused and in considerable pain. Suddenly I felt a massive blow to the side of my head, horrendous nausea ...

And then nothing but blackness.

The White House

Two days later - Washington DC, USA.

FRED M. VINSON, CHIEF JUSTICE OF THE AMERICAN FEDERAL GOVERNMENT walked into Alexander Duvall's office without knocking. Vinson's face was etched with concern, expression grim. Duvall was head of Internal Security, a personal appointee of President Truman.

"We've got a shed load of problems in the UK, Alex. It concerns a US Army detachment and a crooked Colonel." He spoke with a Kentucky accent and gestured over his shoulder. "The President wants you to handle it. He'll be right along." He sat down heavily in Duvall's visitor chair and stared at him: "This is just a heads up, before he gets here."

"Go on," said Duvall, immediately fascinated. He was a handsome man, with blue eyes and the build of an athlete.

"Does the name Brimblecombe sound familiar?" The voice was almost sing-song in its delivery: "Professor Nicholas

Brimblecombe?"

Duvall glanced down at the pages of his leather-bound diary as if they might provide an insight: "Sure. British Intelligence. The dark shadow of European Ops our boys used to call him in WW2. Rumour has it he sneaked an MI6 spy right at the top of Nazi High Command. Never confirmed or admitted. Scuttlebutt, I guess. Why?"

Vinson sniffed: "Brimblecombe called Truman about the Army problem. Apparently Brimblecombe has their Prime Minister's full approval. The man has contacts that span the globe. I bet he has a guy in the Kremlin." The last comment was a joke, but it fell flat.

"Go on," said Duvall again, imagining scenarios and opportunities; he was always on the lookout for the upper hand.

"An English ATS girl has been murdered in London. And Brimblecombe knows American Military are behind it. Says he has irrefutable evidence."

"Good God!"

One short rap on the door announced Truman's arrival. It was a warning, not a courtesy. With his rimless glasses and receding hairline he had more the look of a doctor than a president. The two men rose as Truman walked in and spoke without preamble:

"We're planning to give millions of dollars in aid to Europe and now this." His glare was accusing, his Missouri accent – as always – strongest when he was up against it. He leant on Duvall's desk. "The hell we gonna do, Alex? Got any ideas?"

Duvall smiled with charm, his voice loaded with positivity: "Not yet, sir. But I will. Be sure of that."

Truman nodded sharply but said nothing.

*

"Is Mrs. Duvall not at home, Maria?" Duvall held the telephone receiver close to his ear. He could picture his Spanish housekeeper in her green apron, standing in the hallway of his elegant Georgetown mansion. His was the most impressive-looking property on Olive Street by a mile. The hundred-year-old building was light and airy, no expense spared in one of the prime locations in DC. Stella Duvall was senior partner at a leading DC law firm; always busy.

"No, Señor Duvall. She's in court today." There was a hint of the Mexican accent she was trying so hard to lose. Mrs. Duvall had paid for elocution because she valued Maria's loyalty and discretion.

"Ok, Maria. Have her call me please, the moment she returns home. I won't bother her now. But I have to go over to England, and I don't know for how long. I'll need two cases packed. Laundered shirts, suits, etcetera. Can you see to it, please?"

Maria said that she would have everything ready by five that evening. Duvall sat back, clasped his hands behind his head and wondered what Stella was really up to. She certainly wasn't in court that day, for sure, so no point in leaving a message with a stranger.

A tap on his office door broke his reverie and an attractive secretary walked in and closed the door softly behind her. She placed travel documents on his desk, leant over and kissed him on the mouth. It was immediate, sensual and intimate. Duvall looked up at her, then his watch.

"I'm gonna miss you, Alex."

Duvall grinned broadly: "I'll be back, Laura. Then we'll go to Hawaii and soak in the ocean, like I promised."

She purred: "Promise again."

The Speaker

St. Ermin's Hotel, St. James's Park, London, England.

ST. ERMIN'S HOTEL was a favourite meeting place for the British Intelligence Services and was notably the birthplace of the SOE. During the 1930's the hotel and the buildings at 2 Caxton Street were used by officers of the SIS, located close by at 54 Broadway. In addition, the hotel was regularly frequented by SIS, MI5 and the Naval Intelligence Division (NID) to recruit spies for operations overseas.

On this particular evening in May, a significant meeting was taking place and its attendees had been invited for a reason. The initial greeting had taken place at the front desk of the hotel – by anonymous civil servants – and guests ushered to the Caxton Hall next door. A stern notice on the door announced:

PRIVATE RECEPTION
BY INVITATION ONLY.

*

The four former secret agents were sitting in the hall, transfixed. Other members of the small audience were equally absorbed by the words of the speaker.

Professor Nicholas Brimblecombe stood at the podium and had opened the talk by telling them how delighted he was they were able to attend his retirement evening. 'Informal' he had said, before the lights had been slightly lowered and the ambience made more intimate. He addressed them thoughtfully for nearly an hour. He was charming and clearly knowledgeable about his subject: war. More specifically, the consequences of war.

He spoke about tyranny, conflict and how near they had come to the end of the civilised world. Nothing he said was new, but it was very engaging; no state secrets were spilt. He discussed D Day, Overlord, atomic weapons and the Japanese surrender. He articulated further on Europe: resistance, occupation, mass-murder and capitulation. Finally, he turned to the craft of spying, a subject four particular people were extremely interested in.

But strangely, he made no mention of the Valentines Cup or Crimson Wing, the ops to which the former spies had been assigned by him. Similarly, the French 'F' Section networks – *réseaux* – SCIENTIST and WHEELWRIGHT were also omitted.

The speaker was convincing. In fact, he was everything a good speaker should be. Except he was not Professor Nicholas Brimblecombe. He was an impostor, and that was why there was no mention of the covert ops: he knew nothing about them.

The former spies realised the fact at once, of course, but chose to say nothing. So, who was this man posing as Brim and why was he there? More importantly, where was the real Brim, the former head of British Intelligence, the spymaster who had guided and mentored the spies through the dark days of the 1940's?

At the end of the speech the man was quickly whisked away by some sort of security agents. Not police, nor army; perhaps a private militia. The audience gradually trickled out of the main exit; they resembled minor civil servants, Foreign Office, perhaps, or MOD. Clement Atlee's Labour Government had had a narrow majority and there had been a lot of reshuffling in the corridors of Whitehall. Not one face was familiar to any of them.

Joselyn Foster, arguably the most vociferous of the four, shot out of her seat the moment 'Brim' disappeared behind a curtain like some Victorian magician in a conjuring act. She approached one of the militia. Her American accent did little to disguise her anger:

"That man," she said breathlessly, "is not Nicholas Brimblecombe."

"And you are ...?" the man asked her in a condescending,

Home Counties tone. He was broad-shouldered with sharp blue eyes and thin lips.

Alistair, Freddie Valentine, together with his wife Astrid, joined the escalating kerfuffle. Alistair took the lead, radiating his natural charm with a winning smile.

"Good evening," he said, making eye contact with the man. "We all worked for Professor Brimblecombe during the war."

"The war ended over a year ago," the man stated resolutely and in a manner which suggested – and it is irrelevant now.

"And we all agree with our colleague," said Freddie, ignoring the man's barb. "The person who addressed us is not Professor Brimblecombe. But we would like to speak to him all the same. If you don't mind."

"That will not be possible." Another man had joined them now: tall, authoritative, regular army or perhaps air force. "The Professor has now left Caxton Hall and returned to a private residence, under guard ..." He paused and looked at the four former spies, one by one, as if committing each of their faces to memory ...

"You have heard the Professor speak, enjoyed a welcome glass of sherry at St. Ermin's. And now it is time to leave." Two more men joined the group, hands inside their jackets, as if grasping for weapons.

Alistair took Joselyn's arm: "Under guard? Oh well, we must have made a mistake."

Joselyn was chomping at the bit; did not want to back down. But Freddie verbally agreed with Alistair and suggested that they should leave as instructed. He noticed that the other members of the audience had also left; the hall was now empty.

The former spies turned to leave, each with their own private thoughts, but one collective notion: that they would get to the bottom of this, no matter what.

*

Later, Alistair, Joselyn, Freddie and Astrid were sitting in a large comfortable suite at the Ritz Hotel. The earlier pots of tea had been replaced by bottles of Liebfraumilch and Mateus Rosé, as they discussed the quandary they were all facing. Room service had also provided roast beef and mustard sandwiches, but such luxuries did little to assuage their predicament.

"So, we agree that the speaker was not Brim," said Alistair, stating the obvious, but kicking off the debate he knew would get them all involved.

"Either he's been kidnapped, or something else." Astrid, although a fluent English speaker, seldom used the language. And 'something' sounded more like sum-sing, but the last two words had a sinister tone to them, all the same.

"Like what?" asked Freddie. "Why would he invite us ... if it's not him?"

Alistair was sitting on the arm of a settee, sipping his wine: "Right. Let's just all think about this. What do we really know?"

"About Brim?" one of the girls asked.

"Yes." Alistair looked at them, his expression serious.

It was Freddie who responded: "Nothing. We don't know where he lives, other than perhaps Pimlico. Because that is what he told us. We know nothing about him."

The former spies looked at each other; it was true. No matter how ridiculous it sounded, these were the facts: Brimblecombe had no wife or family that any of them had ever heard about. Or even close friends. He was an enigma. But in a way, that was the point. As head of British Intelligence, he had had to be remote.

"Miss Trueblood, his secretary?" Astrid asked. Miss Trueblood was a legend in the Service: similarly remote, sapient and utterly devoted to Brimblecombe.

"Retired. Her whereabouts unknown because of Official Secrets?" Freddie suggested, not sure where she was.

"Ingrid and Manfred?"

Astrid confirmed that her parents had been visiting Hong Kong and Singapore since the end of the war. Letters had been sent to her and Freddie at Chalet Monte Rosa, but they hadn't spoken; phone connections to south-east Asia were dubious at the best of times.

"And my father now works for the US State Department in

Paris," said Joselyn. Charles Foster had been the American Ambassador in London until he'd met and fallen in love with a French anaesthetist, after his wife had died. As she and Alistair now spent much of their time in Massachusetts, the shock of his romance had dulled.

"Mr. Churchill? He and Brim were confidants during the DAS SCHLOSS case. But he's out of Government and official channels are most probably closed." Alistair slipped off the sofa and wandered over to the window.

"There is one other person," Freddie reminded them: a delicate subject. "Sally Brooke. She and Brim are distantly related. If there's one person who might know where Brim is, it is she."

"Last we heard," said Alistair, "she was working in the Anaesthetics Department at St. Mary's Hospital, here in London. Paddington. Isn't that right, Freddie?"

Freddie looked sheepish. He and Sally had been more than good friends a few years back, before he had met and married Astrid. Astrid knew the story, but the subject was generally off-limits these days. Alistair grinned at his brother:

"It would be a decent walk from here to Paddington, Freddie. Maybe I'll join you in the morning? Let's go and investigate, it will be like the old days. You know when we were real spies."

Alistair And Joselyn

One month earlier
Copley Hotel, Copley Square, Boston, USA

COPLEY SQUARE IN THE BACK BAY area of Boston was a thriving hub of commerce and culture. Its architecture and style dated back to the 1860's and had a feeling of understated American affluence: the square was wide, with grassy sections on which people sat and watched the world go by. The Copley Hotel or Copley, as it was universally known, was a recently refurbished building on the Trinity Church side.

The lobby was bustling with life: tourists, locals and businesspeople. Its walls were adorned with signed photographs of Red Sox baseball players of the past: Babe Ruth; centre fielder Paul DiMaggio and Ted Williams, to name a few. The lobby and reception area smelt of freshly percolated coffee and hot dogs. The vendor, just outside the entrance, had a line of customers waiting. It was as long as Fenway Park Stadium, home to the Red Sox.

Sophie, the receptionist, called the bell-boy, a fully liveried hotel porter: green suit, cap and shiny brass buttons. A bountiful show of tips had given him a bright smile and plenty of hope about romance.

"Letter from England," Sophie called out to him. "Take it up to Mr. and Mrs. Valentines' suite. They're staying in the Plaza suite. Top floor."

"Sure, Sofe." He smiled at her charmingly, but to no avail. One day, he thought, one day I will summon the courage to ask her out.

The bellboy stood in the staff-only elevator and gazed at the airmail envelope; it was a sight he had never seen before: handwritten, postmarked London, April 1st. The item had been rubber-stamped: RECEIVED US MAIL.

He rang the doorbell of the Valentines' sumptuous suite and waited.

*

Alistair Valentine slit the flimsy envelope open with his wife Joselyn's Swiss Army Knife and strolled out onto the spacious balcony overlooking the square. He read the contents and called out:

"Honey!" Alistair, though English and raised in Zermatt, Switzerland, had adopted this curious Americanism. It had initially irritated Joselyn, but now she had 'gotten used to it.' She padded barefoot across the plush carpeted lounge towards him.

Bright morning sunlight shone in through the huge balcony windows. She blinked, momentarily dazzled. Joselyn had a sensuous, wide mouth, full lips and dimpled cheeks when she smiled. Which she often did. A look of detached amusement was her natural expression. Her face, though not classically beautiful, was alluring and noble, like an exquisitely crafted work of art. Her deep-blue eyes did, however, betray her mood: fire and fury one moment, deep serenity the next. She walked to the balcony door, wearing a towelling bathrobe, her hair wrapped up in a towel.

"It better be important," she said in her husky Massachusetts voice.

"It's an invitation to Brim's retirement evening. St. Ermin's Hotel in London. The home of the Intelligence fraternity. I met him there a few times. Quite apt, really."

"When is it?"

"June."

"Is he sixty? Isn't that when you guys get your gold watch and chain? Or in his case, long service medal?"

"This is serious, Joss."

"When in June?"

Alistair read her the full contents of the airmail letter. She made various faces as she absorbed the information: where they might stay and for how long; options for travel.

"I guess Freddie and Astrid will be invited, right?" The sentence came out in typical east-coast syntax; hard to decipher whether it was a question or a statement.

He looked her in the eye: "There's no reason in the world why they shouldn't be. I'll call him later." Alistair glanced at his watch, calculating the continental Europe time difference. "In about five or six hours, I would guess."

She stepped out through the balcony door and walked over to him, her gown falling open slightly: "There's time then, honey," she said breathlessly, lips parted. "I can do without another sight-seeing trip. What about you?"

Freddie, Astrid, and Christina

One month earlier
Bahnhofplatz, Zermatt, Switzerland.

FREDDIE AND ASTRID WERE walking down the main thoroughfare toward the station and the bottom of the Gornergrat mountain rack-railway. They were wheeling their three-year-old daughter Christina in her pushchair. The summer season was about to start, and the town was beginning to see more tourists. The Alpine sun illuminated the Matterhorn and surrounding mountains of the Valais. A postman darted out of the sorting office toward the few travellers heading for the ticket office.

"Herr Valentine!" the postman called out, clutching an envelope. "This arrived for you from England. Special delivery. Saves me another walk up to Chalet Monte Rosa!" He handed it to Freddie.

"Thank you, Günter," he said with an amused expression.

"Save those legs for the more challenging slopes!"

"Was ist das?" asked Astrid, immediately curious.

Freddie Valentine opened the airmail envelope. It was postmarked London, April 1st. The address was handwritten.

"It's from Brim," said Freddie, speedily reading the contents.

"Aren't you going to share it?" asked Astrid, both surprised and alarmed. A communiqué from London might mean trouble.

Freddie handed Astrid the flimsy airmail letter and she read the few lines carefully before re-folding it and handing it back: "Well?" she said.

"Well, what?" Freddie replied. "Come on, the Zürich train won't wait. And we need to get some coffee and sandwiches for the journey."

He knew well meant she didn't want to go; it would be too much trouble travelling with Christina. They dashed toward the station buffet. Freddie with his curious gait lagged slightly behind, taking out his wallet with a hint of premonition: he knew he faced an expensive day out with his wife and daughter. Shopping in Zürich was more of a habit than a necessity and he had better things to do with his time. And Christina would probably pester them continuously.

Paddington

Present time
St. Mary's Hospital, London, England.

ALISTAIR AND FREDDIE found the Anaesthetics Department at the back of the hospital. It had moved since Freddie had last been there in October 1943. Sally Brooke had had a spell working there on secondment from her nursing job at the Queen Victoria Hospital, East Grinstead.

The new secretary was surprised at the knock on her office door and the sight of two debonair gentlemen apologising for disturbing her. Freddie posed the question.

"Sally Brooke, no. She hasn't worked here for some time." She brushed her chin with a forefinger, face perplexed. "I believe she moved back to Scotland. Yes, that was it, I remember. She married an RAF pilot who'd been shot down in the Channel."

"Do you know where in Scotland, by any chance?" Freddie asked her hopefully.

"No. Such personal details are confidential, hospital policy. Sorry."

Sally

Ritz Hotel Gift Shop, London, England.

"SURPRISED, FREDDIE?"

Sally Brooke's highland lilt was at once recognisable; Freddie turned to see her. She hadn't changed at all. Still the freckled face, lively blue eyes, auburn hair and the beguiling smile that had enchanted him when they'd first met. Freddie was so astounded to see her that he forgot to buy a newspaper and the cuddly toy he had promised for Christina.

"I thought you were married and living in Scotland." It was an unimaginative response but all he could think of.

A flash of sorrow crossed her face: "I was."

"Oh."

"If you must know, Freddie, he didn't compare with you ..."

Now Freddie was speechless.

"... in so many ways." She stopped herself from continuing

and looked at him appealingly. Both of them knew what the other was thinking.

Freddie and Sally had enjoyed a passionate wartime romance. It had begun while he was recuperating at the Queen Victoria Hospital, East Grinstead, in December 1941. Freddie had ditched a Tiger Moth trainer in the Fens and had lost half of his left leg as a result of the accident.

When Freddie had been recruited into British Intelligence in June 1943, his life changed again. His mission had taken him into occupied Europe where he met Astrid Lochar, the love of his life and now the mother of his beloved daughter, Christina. Sally was a remnant from his bachelor past, a glorious memory of love and intimacy. But that was then. This sudden encounter – just a few years on – was alarming because it was so unexpected. Did he still care for her? was all he could think.

"Did you hear what I said, Freddie?"

"Heard and was still processing, I suppose." He looked her in the eye and in that moment a thousand memories flashed through his mind.

She laughed: "Same old Freddie, aye. Evasive."

"Brim?" he asked suddenly, desperate to change the subject.

"Let's find a quiet wee spot in the lounge, Freddie," she said, deftly avoiding his question. Though Astrid, Alistair and Joselyn were upstairs, he found himself following the petite figure as she crossed the carpeted Reception area.

*

Sally made herself comfortable as they sat together on a plump sofa in a corner of the beautifully appointed Ritz lounge. It was late afternoon and there were few guests. The atmosphere was one of understated opulence and elegance, a low hum of hushed voices. Sally turned to Freddie, smoothing down the creases of her tartan plaid skirt, her eyes sparkling with life and undisguised energy. She was ready to talk business:

"Does the name Jessica Hope ring any bells?"

Freddie shook his head and asked about Brim again.

"Bear with me, please," Sally said.

A waiter came over and asked them if they wished to order anything; they both declined. Freddie glanced at his watch. It might have given the impression he was short of time. He was not; he was still shocked at seeing her. And now being so close to her again he felt her warmth and familiar fragrance.

Sally lowered her voice: "What I am about to tell you is top secret and I am only authorised to do so because I have been instructed; and because of who you are."

"Understood." Freddie's pat answer when pressed.

"In September 1941 Jessica was recruited from the ATS and sent to the Government Code and Cypher School at Bletchley Park. The location and its function are highly classified and will be for at least another fifty years. Jessica had no idea why she had been chosen or even where she was, at first ...

Before the train journey from Aldershot to Bletchley, she had been asked by the man who was escorting her – an Army Signals Major - to sign the Official Secrets Act. For the journey by unmarked military transport, from the station to the house, she had been blindfolded and felt unable to protest."

"I can't say I blame her."

But Sally was keen to move on: "After being allowed half a day to settle in she was set to work. Her duties were registering the Morse code messages as they came in from the 'Y' signal stations scattered all over the country ...

The registering of each message by date and call sign order was necessary for the decoders and translators to make quick reference. This was the only part of the message 'in the clear.' The rest was simply groups of five letters or figures. The information was carefully recorded by Jessica and others on index cards. After registration, the messages were decoded, translated, transcribed and assessed according to their urgency and forwarded as appropriate to the Prime Minister and Commanders in the field ..."

"Sally, this is all very well, but ..."

"Bear with me," she said again and referred to notes she had retrieved from her handbag. "In 1943/44 when it became necessary to increase the number of staff in the Japanese Section she was transferred to Block 'F' at BP. She was paraphrasing already-translated Japanese messages. It was considered a precaution to paraphrase messages they had intercepted and decoded. These concerned details of impending Japanese troop movements in Burma. But much more important were messages sent by Japanese Generals – based in Berlin – back to Tokyo. Information concerning the inspection of the Atlantic Wall by German and Japanese military; the Germans' thoughts and beliefs about where and when the invasion of Europe would take place."

"Incredible."

"Yes. But more than that. The Intelligence told Mr. Churchill and the Allies not so much what Hitler was thinking – in a way that was obvious – but how he was thinking. Was he convinced about the deception of Calais rather than Normandy?"

Freddie was spellbound by the extent of her knowledge and absorbed the information as she continued, watching his face carefully ...

"Bletchley Park had to be sure the Japanese didn't realise their Intelligence had been compromised and their codes had been broken."

"That makes sense. Go on."

"It was complex, but Jessica was bright and naturally adept. After three years of working and living at BP, her talents were recognised by her superiors. She was transferred to the United States. The Pentagon, to be precise."

"Quite an achievement ..."

Sally ignored Freddie's quip. "Jessica's duty was still registering, and paraphrasing translated Japanese Comms. She was quick and efficient in her role. After a while, the Americans gave her a job as a special courier, taking secret papers from one department to another within Washington. The position was not without risk: they trained her in basic field craft and by then she was being paid an additional salary by the US Department of Defence. At the end of the war, after the Japanese surrender, she was discharged."

"Back to Bletchley?"

Sally wrinkled her nose, the way she did and tapped her notes: "No, well, not directly. While she was in Washington, she accidentally stumbled upon a classified document concerning equipment at Bletchley, and this piqued her curiosity."

Freddie frowned: "Equipment at Bletchley?"

"When she returned to England, she immediately travelled up to BP. There, she discovered the work of Codes and Ciphers was still operational."

"Even though the war was over?"

"Yes. As she entered the huts area, she found a number of civilians and WRNS dismantling the wartime decoding equipment: Alan Turing's Bombes and Colossus machines. We now know one was taken to Manchester University for computer research. The remainder were dismantled. This was important as they contained large numbers of thermionic valves, which were in short supply and were needed for other purposes. Some documentary evidence was also destroyed, while other files were moved to GCHQ to be stored in secret."

"And?"

"Jessica knew about combined cipher machines or CCM."

"You've lost me."

"A cipher machine system for securing Allied communications during the war. The British Typex machine and the US ECM were both modified so that they were interoperable, but without all the detail. That information was classified."

"I see."

"One evening she was caught apparently snooping around in one of the huts and was challenged."

Freddie interrupted her: "Was she snooping, though? Or was she entitled to be there? She still had military clearance, presumably."

"Yes, but snooping was Brim's choice of word, and it probably came from Jessica. The point is she had no legitimate reason to be there, yet she was."

"Meaning?" Freddie liked to delve; always had.

"She was on leave. After she left the Pentagon, she sailed back to England on a commandeered cruise ship – Aquitania - with other ATS girls. Her orders were to return to the Aldershot base camp to wait for discharge from the Army – demob – with the rest of the group."

"And she ignored orders?"

"Yes and went straight to BP on a series of trains."

"Because of the classified document which had piqued her curiosity?"

"Yes," she said again.

Freddie chuckled. "Go on. Who challenged her at BP that evening?"

"This is where it gets intriguing. He was an American, dressed in civvies. Although Brim is pretty sure he was a former member of the American 6813th Signal Security Detachment. It was set up to run UK Bombes. So, he would have had inside knowledge about these combined cipher machines and where they were located. At which sites."

"I'm surprised the Americans were involved?"

"Yes. Eighty-five US officers and men. They were billeted in the Manor House at Little Brickhill, a few miles south-east of Bletchley. Cryptanalysts evaluating German traffic."

"Working for Government Code and Cipher School?"

"Yes, or rather working with them. But this was a year later. He should not have been there. Jessica found it a wee bit suspicious."

"It certainly sounds it, Sally."

“Jessica reported the matter to the Military Police; there were still a few on site. They said they would look into it and told her to go home. Which she did.”

“That’s not the end of it?”

“She went to Scotland Yard who immediately put her in contact with the Security Services here in London and ...”

Freddie smiled and looked out of the window onto Piccadilly: “Don’t tell me. Brim got involved.”

“Yes, they had two confidential meetings at Brim’s office and a final one at Lyons Corner House on Shaftesbury Avenue. She handed him documentary evidence and he instructed her not to confide in anyone about anything and to return to her digs on Blackfriars Road and start packing. He said he would send a car for her within the hour so MI5 could re-locate her to a temporary safe house.”

“I sense something is ...”

“Jessica Hope’s body was discovered behind Waterloo Station. A dog walker found her. She had been there no more than an hour according to the Post-Mortem. And that ties in with Brim’s estimation of the timescale. She was identified by fingerprints and dental records; poor girl had no papers on her. And no possessions: no bag or anything, as if she had been robbed. But it was clearly a pre-meditated murder. She had been targeted and killed under orders. But whose?”

“Indeed, whose?”

"There was a massive trauma wound to the side of her head and three broken ribs: pneumothorax. A strange combination of injuries when you think about it. Her parents are heartbroken; they knew nothing of what she had done during the latter war years or even where she worked, because she had signed the Official Secrets Act. She was twenty-four years old."

"That's a poignant story, Sally. But what about Brim?" Freddie's brain had notched up a gear, trying to take it all in. The sad fate of an innocent young girl doing a job for her country.

Sally sighed, her eyes were glassy with moisture: "Brim is under serious threat, Freddie. His Humber staff car exploded unexplained, right outside 54 Broadway. It was as if the perpetrators were trying to warn him – and scare him – that they knew who he was and were onto him. Whatever the motive, he has been forced to go into hiding."

Freddie gulped in shock: "Police?"

"No police involved. The PM's been informed, as has the Home Secretary. The problem is that many of the people within Brim's wartime network have either retired or are dead. And let's face it, he has trampled on a few toes over the years. The situation is desperate. The enemy is unknown."

Freddie sighed: "This is shocking. But how and why did you get involved in all of this?"

"Brim's direct orders. You know I've always been under his Intelligence umbrella, don't you, Freddie?"

Freddie raised his eyebrows: "Not this closely. Did you organise the fake retirement party and the fake Brim?"

Sally's beguiling smile was back, but only for a second. The smile said yes, but she didn't admit it: "He can't trust anyone, Freddie. Do you know of Brigadier Sir Cyril Downing, MI5?"

"Brim spoke of him back in '43. Downing and Churchill were both connected to the mission Alistair and I were involved in."

"He is on side, of course, but extremely cautious. This sort of thing is unprecedented. Brim is a wanted man because of what Jessica Hope had confided in him: that she believed the precious decoding machines had been stolen by persons unknown; possibly American. That's really it, in a nutshell."

There was a sudden flurry of activity. Alistair, Joselyn and Astrid came into the quiet section of the Ritz lounge. There you are they all seemed to say in unison. What they saw was: Freddie quietly ensconced on a cosy sofa with his ex-lover, an attractive auburn-haired lady wearing a tartan plaid skirt and a broad smile.

Astrid did not have to admonish him because the look on her face was self-evident. The situation was awkward. Alistair instinctively took the lead and gave Freddie and Sally his winning smile: "Well, Freddie. Aren't you going to introduce us?"

*

The table in the Ritz Bar was adorned with tall glasses of iced gin and tonic, homemade potato crisps and peanuts. Sally and Freddie had explained the tragic fate of Jessica Hope and outlined her belief that a conspiracy – of some sort – had taken place at BP in those final days.

They continued the conversation in hushed tones. It was Joselyn who spoke first:

"I understand all you have said, Sally. And I can see why Brim has gone into hiding. But why stage the fake retirement reception at St. Ermin's? What was its purpose?" Her Massachusetts tone accentuated the last word.

Sally deliberated before answering: "The evening had been planned ages ago by Miss Trueblood. The point is, not many people in the corridors of Whitehall know what Brim actually looks like. The audience at Caxton Hall the other night would have been none the wiser. If the place were being watched – which we are sure it was – the evening could carry on as normal. Don't they call it 'keeping up appearances?'"

Freddie interjected with a grin: "While the real Brim is in hiding, planning his next move."

"Which is what, exactly?" Joselyn asked. Alistair could sense Joselyn's distrust of Sally because she felt for Astrid: Sally appeared to be a threat.

Sally sipped her long drink with undisguised relish: "To meet you all, of course. What else? I am his special envoy."

Astrid tapped Freddie on the leg: "I'll have to return to Switzerland. Christina will be starting to miss me. We can't leave the babysitter with her for too long."

A flash of something crossed Sally's face and the only one who spotted it, as always, was Alistair.

Sally looked at the group: "Security for the evening was overseen by Miles Villiers from the RAF Special Investigation Branch – SIB/North/Cranwell. Freddie, I believe you know Group Captain Villiers?"

"I have met him a couple of times at Brim's office, yes. I don't particularly know him as such."

"Anyway," continued Sally, "Villiers and the boffins at 'Churchill's Toy Shop' had devised a room full of booby traps and explosives should there have been any trouble."

Sally was referring to Churchill's secret military defence laboratory (MD1), a unit in the village of Whitchurch in Buckinghamshire, also known as The Firs. Here British Intelligence technicians created everything from miniature radios and silk rag-tissue maps to incendiary devices for sabotaging railway depots in occupied France. And magnetic limpet mines for sinking U-Boats.

"But that need didn't arise," said Alistair, glancing at Freddie and the others.

"Aye," Sally agreed. "But the point is both Villiers and MD1 are available to you, if need be."

Joselyn, still irritated about the Sally/Astrid dynamic said: "And will the need be, do you think? You seem to know all the answers."

Sally ignored the barb. Instead, her face broke into a captivating smile that was impossible to ignore: "I would think it was inevitable, wouldn't you, Joselyn?"

Beckworth

Comms/Intelligence
The Pentagon, Virginia, USA.

COLONEL JOHN BECKWORTH LOOKED GRIM. He was sitting at his desk, his clenched fist clutching a telephone receiver. His normal jovial expression and animated demeanour had melted into a mask of concern.

"You're saying this is a renegade group of US military, gone AWOL in UK?"

The caller had introduced himself as a Major in the US Army - and explained that the soldiers in question – the 6813th Signals Security Detachment based at Bletchley Park – had been missing for nearly a week. He thought Beckworth might be interested to know.

"How many men are we talking about here, Major?" Beckworth's insincerity was hidden well.

"Three." was the reply. "And the Brits are saying a number of combined cipher machines have vanished, as well as highly secret documentation."

"And do they believe the Pentagon has something to do with it?" Again, the tone sounded sincere. Beckworth was doodling with a pencil in his opened diary- cum-dossier. He had already crossed out a number of scheduled appointments for that morning. The caller next explained that a young English ATS girl named Jessica Hope had been murdered in London.

Beckworth swallowed deeply, the cartilage of his Adam's apple became even more prominent: "A Jessica Hope from Bletchley Park worked here for God's sake. I knew her. It can't be the same girl, surely to hell?"

The caller, who sounded educated and authoritative confirmed that it was. And the receiver slid down Beckworth's stubbled jawline. Beckworth was forty-two and married with a family; Jessica was twenty-four and single. Their affair had been intense and passionate. It was Beckworth who had caught Jessica photographing the classified document from the Pentagon.

He could not, would not, report the matter, although he clearly should have. But he had a vested interest in not only keeping the matter quiet but getting rid of her at the earliest opportunity. That way he would still have control of the situation.

"Colonel Beckworth? Are you still there?" The caller raised

his voice, not sure whether or not the Colonel had heard the final portion of the grim news.

"Yes, yes, sorry. I am .... what's that?" Beckworth put the receiver back to his ear and swallowed once again as he listened.

"Professor Brimblecombe of British Intelligence holds you responsible, not only for her death but also for the missing cipher machines. And he claims he has evidence. Be sure I will be in touch."

The line went dead. The caller was not a Major in the US Army. He was Alexander Duvall from the White House. And as head of Internal Security, he could do more or less as he pleased.

Alice

Blakeney Quay, Norfolk, England.

MISS ALICE TRUEBLOOD was clearly the lady of the manor. Her home – Gunfleet – was a substantial brick and flint-built house with connections to maritime trading and seafaring which dated back more than two hundred years. Its imposing presence overlooked Blakeney Quay and the vast salt marshes beyond. The feel of the property and grounds was distinctly nautical, with a rusty old anchor wedged in the mud at water's edge. The 'look out' window of the second storey had unimpeded views of Blakeney Point, Pinchen's Creek and the sea in the distance. An antique telescope, mounted centrally, bore testament to Gunfleet's clandestine history: a vantage point that had served many purposes over the years. Black-headed gulls were omnipresent – and had been from time immemorial – hovering and sweeping above the sloping gardens down to Gunfleet's private mooring.

Alice was a tall, angular woman in her sixties. She spoke with a distinct, clipped English accent, that belied her uncanny ability with foreign languages. Her clothing, though of obvious quality, was dowdy and plain. Since her father, Admiral Charles Trueblood, had passed away, matters concerning the running of Gunfleet had fallen to her. It was a position she relished. For the first time in her life, she had acquired independent wealth and the freedom such an inheritance brings. She oversaw and managed a small fishing fleet which brought a modest income to the Gunfleet estate. Her maritime responsibility extended to Cley-next-the-Sea, Salthouse and Weybourne. And a group of Norfolk fishermen who held her in high esteem.

Alice's pride and joy was a Matthew's Motor Yacht 38 Sedan. The forty-foot craft was constructed of wood and powered by twin 6-Cylinder petrol engines. The M.Y. GUNFLEET was moored in the Port of Harwich, because of Admiral Trueblood's close association with HMS Ganges nearby. The Royal Navy kept a close eye on her and made sure the tarpaulin was carefully secured after each voyage Alice made. She was competent with the craft, but it ideally needed two extra hands for a voyage of any length.

After a thirty-year career with British Intelligence and a tiny flat on Wigmore Street, she was back in the place where she had been raised and learned how to sail and catch fish. Gunfleet was now very much Alice's domain, although she had retained all her father's antique furniture and artworks.

Since before the war, she'd been personal assistant to Professor Nicholas Brimblecombe, head of British Intelligence. Her position at the St. James's Park offices had brought her into the company and trust of the Prime Minister, Chiefs of Staff and senior members of the Armed Forces. Throughout the war she had been no stranger to the hallowed areas of the Admiralty Citadel, Churchill's War Rooms and Number Ten. Throughout August and September 1943, she had been Brim's confidante in the events leading up to the operation the Nazis had named DAS SCHLOSS.

In August of this year, Jessica Hope had walked into Brim's office with a file under her arm. She was petite, highly attractive and spoke in a voice that had the slightest hint of an American intonation.

"Hi," she had said with an almost confident flamboyance, "I've an appointment with Professor Brimblecombe at noon; I guess I'm a little early."

Those few words were destined to change the lives of the three of them. Part of Alice Trueblood's last job had been to organise the faux evening at the St. Ermin's Hotel and Caxton Hall. There was a sharp knock on her kitchen door, a familiar tattoo that was also a signal. As she greeted him, her visitor looked at his watch. A dapper fellow, casually attired, eloquently spoken and not given to small talk.

"Hello, Alice," said Brim. "You remember Group Captain

Villiers, don't you?"

"Yes, come in, Miles. I'll make some coffee. Earl Grey for you, Brim?"

Brim pursed his lips, the way he did: "No milk or sugar, please, Alice. But then, you know that by now."

Alice turned her lean frame to the Aga: "Make yourselves at home in the snug. I'll bring it through. There have been one or two developments since we last spoke, Brim. My contact in Whitehall has been busy."

Villiers raised his eyebrows at Brim with an expression which said: whatever could happen next?

*

Alice poured Brim's Earl Grey from a china teapot into a cup and daintily popped a slice of lemon in with sugar tongs. Miles Villiers sipped coffee from a sturdy-looking mug and watched the procedure with amusement. He detected a familiarity between them which suggested an understanding he found rather endearing. Alice addressed them both with level, serious eyes:

"The 6813th Detachment consisted of eighty-five US personnel at GC&CS. This included SIXTA for traffic analysis, Hut 6 for cryptanalysis of the Enigma machine, Block F for cryptanalysis of FISH traffic and Hut 3 for evaluation and exploitation of German traffic ..."

Brim and Villiers listened intently as Alice continued after a slight pause. "My contact in Whitehall reports that of the original eighty-five US personnel only eighty-two are now accounted for. There have been three separate roll calls on the two Navy carriers returning to America."

Brim pursed his lips in thought: "Three missing then?"

Alice picked up a cardboard file, donned a pair of pince-nez and scanned the confidential US ARMY document:

"Yes. Captains Mendoza, Darville and Boseman, all unaccounted for, as is the Comms equipment they purloined from BP. Plus service manuals."

"Boseman?" Villiers asked her again, cautiously.

"The soldiers' surnames are all synonymous with the southern states of America. The Gulf Coast, so I am persuaded to believe."

Brim took out his distinctive silver cigarette case and lit a non-tipped Senior Service with his battered old Ronson:

"Colonel John Beckworth was from Florida, if I recall," said Brim inhaling deeply. "It was a detail Jessica confided. Pensacola, on the coast."

"I've visited that area," Villiers said expansively, "Mobile, Biloxi, Gulfport and New Orleans. Fabulous places, all of them."

"So, it is more than possible," Alice said, ignoring Villiers's travelogue, “that Beckworth and these three captains knew one another.”

Brim stubbed out his cigarette irritably and stood. He walked over to the ‘look-out’ window and glanced across at Blakeney Point, tapping the old telescope in thought.

“What was it Jessica showed us that first day, Alice? The photograph she had taken at the office in the Pentagon together with the incriminating letter from Beckworth.”

“Yes.”

“I think she and Beckworth were having more than the casual romance she alluded to. For her, it was very serious. He refused to leave his wife and family for her. And certainly not to jeopardise his position at the Pentagon. That was the real reason why she came to see me: plain vindictiveness.”

Villiers sighed: “To inform on him, you mean?”

“A woman spurned ...” said Brim to the window, his back still turned.

Miss Trueblood, embarrassed at such a perfidious notion, cleared her throat judiciously: “Circumstantial evidence, Brim. With respect.”

“As I said the other day, Alice. I hold Beckworth responsible for her murder and I stand by that conclusion.” He turned from the window to face them; the ritual was reminiscent of a courtroom drama.

Villiers pulled a long face which turned down the corners of his mouth in doubt: "Is it conceivable an American Colonel, based in the Pentagon, could organise the murder of a girl in Waterloo. I mean, is that a credible possibility?"

His tone was doubtful, but his game was to get Brim to develop his argument. And Brim knew the ploy well. He returned to his seat and sat down more heavily than he had intended.

"Possibly not," he responded, brushing imaginary flecks of ash from his perfectly pressed trousers. "But our three renegades could. That's more than a possibility."

"If they were all in cahoots," replied Villiers slowly, as if the light were dawning.

"Let me pose a question, Miles. How are three unscrupulous American deserters going to be able to sell what is very obviously stolen government technology to a third party?"

"Not the Army?"

"No, Miles. Not the Army. They already have a degree of computer technology – and let's face it – the American Army APO 413 – have been working with Bletchley Park. So, they have some of the answers, but not all."

"A commercial organisation?"

"Yes." A lightbulb moment which made Villiers appear stupid, although Brim hadn't intended it as such.

"The point is our renegades need a go-between to represent their interests."

"A negotiator, you mean?" asked Villiers.

"I prefer go-between. But yes, an intermediary to broker some kind of a deal. This middleman would act on behalf of the three men to persons unknown."

Villiers bit his lip and regarded Miss Trueblood with unseeing eyes, his mind elsewhere, digesting the information into some composite form.

"Are you suggesting Colonel John Beckworth engineered this whole scenario in the first place and these soldiers were merely acting on his behalf?"

Brim remained silent; seconds elapsed as Villiers continued: "That's why Jessica Hope was killed. She found out. And wanted more evidence against him than she already had."

Brim slurped the remains of his cold tea: "It's why I am enjoying the salt marshes of Blakeney and not sitting at my desk in St. James's. They're onto me."

Villiers suddenly looked sheepish: "That brings me to the main reason why I wanted to come up here and see you, Brim. Thank you, by the way, for the use of your driver, Captain Clitheroe. Good man."

For a brief moment Brim smiled: "Alistair, Freddie and

Joselyn are at the Ritz. Yes, Sally sent me a telegram. They're awaiting my instructions."

"Charles Wighton, the man who stood in for you at St. Ermin's ... your retirement evening."

"What about him?" But even as he asked the question, he knew the answer.

"Found dead at the Marylebone apartment."

"My God."

"Someone must have followed him from Caxton Hall."

Brim suddenly looked pale: "He was under guard though? Your men from SIB/North/Cranwell?"

"Yes. They escorted him to the apartment – saw him in safely – and left. They waited outside the apartment block for over an hour in an unmarked car. Everything seemed quiet."

A whirl of notions passed through Brim's mind: never underestimate the enemy; don't take any chances; double check. All useless now; an innocent civilian – with a passing resemblance to himself – killed in cold blood. Right under their noses.

"How?" was the only word Brim could summon.

Villiers sighed: "Same as Jessica: a massive trauma wound to the side of Wighton's head and three broken ribs, pneumothorax. He put up a hell of a fight, but at his age he was no match for his attacker ..."

Brim raised his eyebrows and pursed his lips, acknowledging the bitter irony: "Bloody hell, Miles."

"The ribs were most probably broken by the strike of an elbow – a well-known combat technique – and deadly."

"Are the police ..."

"No. I contacted Cyril Downing, MI5. Your old colleague was shocked. But this is a domestic concern."

"Do Alistair and Freddie know about this yet?"

Villiers shook his head: "I thought it best to see you first, in person."

"Get back to London, Miles. Quick as you can and put them in the picture."

Villiers rose: "I feel dreadful about this, Brim. Wighton's security was my responsibility. We took a lot of precautions at Caxton Hall, just in case."

But it was Alice who responded: "The measure of the opposition is now abundantly clear, Miles. You mustn't blame your team. Or yourself."

Villiers nodded, unconvinced, and left the 'look-out' room. Moments later an engine started, and the car sped away from Gunfleet barely an hour after it had arrived. Brim watched out of the window; his expression was grim; but he was also a realist. Charles Wighton's untimely death had at least bought him time. And that was what he needed most.

Deserters

Petticoat Lane. East London, England.

"AMERICAN BUSINESS MACHINES have offered our mediator quarter of a million bucks for these beauties." The man glanced at two cipher machines, a British Typex and several stepping mechanisms.

There were also two bulky manuals marked: GOVERNMENT CODE AND CIPHER SCHOOL – Bletchley Park – DO NOT REMOVE. Another folder was marked FISH; the codename given at BP to German teleprinter traffic encrypted using the Lorenz SZ40/42 cipher machines. The TYPEX was the British rotor-based cipher machine, used for encryption of Allied messages, as an analogue for Enigma during the decryption process. A UK map of Y STATIONS identified the wireless intercept stations located around the UK and overseas.

The man announcing this colossal theft was Captain Larry Boseman. And although born in Mobile, Alabama, his accent did not betray his southern roots. Boseman's father had been in the US Army and much of Boseman's youth had been spent stationed overseas.

The three deserters sitting in a disused Marconi warehouse near Petticoat Lane, east London, were the renegades from 6813th Signal Security Detachment US ARMY. These were the Army captains – Mendoza, Darville and Boseman – whom Alice had mentioned to Brim and Villiers. They all originated from the Gulf coast of America.

The latter was the figure head and spokesman for the deserters: a natural leader; well-travelled and more sophisticated than the others. None of them – except him - had washed properly or shaved for a week. There were discarded rations of tinned food and empty beer bottles scattered around. The three men shared one toilet and a sink that had been used to clean machine parts in former years. The single bar of British army-issue soap had seen better days.

"ITC'll pay more," said Brad Darville. "Quarter of a mill is chicken shit."

Boseman went over to Darville, bent down and punched him playfully on the shoulder: "Oh really? The hell you know about anything, soldier? You know nothing about ITC or ABM." He became serious: "I'm the one who spoke to our mediator. Not you."

"Sure, Larry. I was just sayin' is all."

Boseman straightened up: “Just remember.”

“Yeah, Larry, but we can’t be too greedy,” offered Mendoza with a smirk. He didn’t mean it, of course. He wanted as much as he could get. They all did. They had risked their lives for the outside possibility of success. The word of one man who had promised them the earth, while taking no personal risk at all.

Boseman eyed his compatriots with an air of informed superiority: “The way I see it, we hold all the aces here. ABM are the ones who are greedy. We are merely innocent facilitators for the Colonel.”

The others chuckled at this understatement. Boseman continued: “If ABM want to get ahead of the Brits in what Flowers calls – computers – they’ll pay, alright. And we’ll be rich. I’m sick of the army and sick of this damn country. I can’t wait to get on that ship in Southampton and go home.”

“Me too, Larry,” said Darville.

Mendoza who was half Mexican, lit a Lucky Strike with his Zippo, flicking the flint wheel against his Army trouser fatigues: “At least that nosey bitch Jessica is out of the way. She could have been a pain in the ass.”

Boseman sneered: “And to think the Colonel was screwing her all the time we were in training. Not that I blame him.”

“What about you then?” asked Mendoza, licking his lips. “Did you? She worked at the Pentagon long enough. And I know your reputation with the ladies. Larry Boseman is a legend, right?”

Boseman smiled at Mendoza: “No comment, Mendoza.”

Brad Darville looked at Boseman: “Pity she had to die.”

Villiers

St. Ermin's Hotel
St. James's Park, London, England.

MILES VILLIERS'S CAR pulled up outside the garden courtyard entrance to the hotel which looked resplendent in the late afternoon sunshine. The vehicle was a 1938 Humber Snipe Imperial, grey and inconspicuous. Villiers climbed out energetically and thanked Brim's driver, Captain Clitheroe, for making the long roundabout journey from London to Blakeney and back again. Clitheroe had been Brim's factotum throughout the war years and was a trusted member of his entourage. Even so, he knew nothing of who was taking refuge at Gunfleet. Or the reason for Villiers's brief visit.

Clitheroe said simply: "Sir." And Villiers walked gingerly into the foyer of the hotel, looking around as if expecting somebody who was late.

'Eliot Ness' and the muscular young man who had caused

Jessica's pneumothorax were sitting in a black Hillman, parked across the road from the courtyard. The muscular young man – Leo – had a pair of high-powered binoculars pressed to his eyes. Considering his appearance and general demeanour he spoke surprising well.

"That's the security man who was at Caxton Hall the other night. Something to do with the late Professor Brimblecombe. What's he doing back here again, I wonder?"

"Villiers," said the other man, who was named simply Travis. Leo and Travis always worked as a team. And street work was their speciality. Four years and thirty 'strikes' and they had never been caught. When Captain Larry Boseman had approached them at the Salmon and Ball pub in the East End, their instructions were clear. Yes, it was a woman and yes, it had to be quick. Boseman had paid well. In cash. And in advance. Travis and Leo liked that. A fat wad of money and no questions asked – just a job – no matter who or why.

"What are we going to do?" asked Leo, clenching his jaw muscles.

"Watch the hotel was Boseman's instruction, for another hundred quid. See who comes and goes and make a note of anyone we might recognise from that retirement evening. Brimblecombe was high-ranking British Intelligence. This hotel is where all the spies go, apparently. Recruitment, interviews ..." He paused ... "So here we are, watching."

"I wouldn't mind being a spy," Leo said. "I'm obviously pretty talented at surveillance. And I can handle myself in a fight."

"You'd stick out like a sore thumb. You'd be bloody useless."

"There's a woman now, look. Quite short, but what a figure. I love that auburn hair. I wonder if she's married." Leo handed Travis the binoculars. "Feast your eyes on that little sweetheart."

"Who cares if she's married or not?"

*

Sally Brooke walked into the hotel but took no notice of Villiers who was standing just outside as if he was waiting for a date to arrive. To the casual onlooker, they were unconnected. Strangers. But that was how Brim had instructed them to be. 'Don't be counted,' he had said to Sally on the telephone earlier. 'Assume you are being observed by our adversaries. Let's try and draw them out. God knows, we need something.'

*

Villiers quickly turned into the hotel as if checking for something and then made a 'sh' sign to Sally and with a glance, subtly gestured her towards the bar.

*

"What?" Sally grinned and frowned at the same time: an expression which more or less defined her. She looked up at Villiers, her eyes sparkling with mischief: sometimes he does take himself terribly seriously, she thought.

Villiers sighed through clenched teeth: "There's a black Hillman parked over across the courtyard with two men in it. I'm sure they were both here the night Charles Wighton was killed. They look as though they're up to no good because they're trying to look casual. It's not working. They're obvious."

"What do you want me to do?" She strained to look at the Hillman but couldn't quite see it from where she was.

"Go to the courtesy phone at reception. Call Alistair and Freddie at the Ritz. This is the number and instruction." Villiers handed Sally a hastily scribbled note. His desperate expression said: read out this message and they will know what to do. Alistair can get what he needs from the staff quarters at the rear of the hotel. There's a service door."

Sally's eyes flashed: "Urgent?"

Villiers smiled: "Yesterday, Sally. Go."

Sally made her way over to reception. The phone was busy, of course. She touched her stomach, suggesting maternal discomfort and looked at the caller with genuine appeal. He hurriedly terminated his call and wordlessly gestured: help yourself.

"Thank you," she said softly.

*

"That man Villiers is going to wear a hole in the street if he stands there any longer. What's he doing?" Travis said, watching from the car.

"Marking time by the look of it. Waiting for someone. Sign of nervous tension. I've seen it before," Leo announced.

"Hello. What's this?"

From the driver's seat, Leo looked in the side-view mirror and saw a man walking purposefully towards their car. He was dressed in a brass-buttoned concierge coat. With his foppish fair hair and athletic physique, he had the look of a matineé idol. Suddenly there was a sharp knock on the driver's side window. Despite Travis and Leo being ready for it, the sheer power of the intrusion startled them both.

"You can't park here," the man said with authority, "we're expecting a limousine from Croydon Airport. Dignitaries."

"Bloody dignitaries," Leo said and pressed the starter. The engine turned over but didn't fire. The man in the coat suddenly grabbed the door handle. It was locked.

Villiers, Sally and Freddie were now on the pavement by the passenger door. Freddie tried the handle, the door was unlocked so he wrenched it open.

"Drive! Drive! Drive!" Travis screamed at Leo. He fumbled with the starter button.

*

Alistair tore off the hotel uniform, rolled it into a bundle around his clenched fist and punched fiercely into the glass. Two more efforts and it shattered: "Get out!" Alistair shouted at Leo.

The passenger door was now open. Villiers was trying to drag Travis out of his seat onto the street. Suddenly the engine fired. Leo jammed the car noisily into gear and stamped on the accelerator. The Hillman roared away with a screech of rubber, leaving the four of them breathless in its wake.

*

Inside the car, Travis said: "That was bloody close. Brimblecombe's lot, I'd guess. So, the woman is part of it along with those two blokes. Brothers I reckon; one has a limp. I noticed it out of the corner of my eye."

Leo turned with a sly grin, failing to see the Police Constable pushing his bike across the road. The sound of the impact was sickening. The officer yelled out in terror. The Hillman was out of control, with the PC and the bike under it.

*

Alistair, Freddie, Sally and Villiers were now running towards the swerving car. Alistair still had the bundled uniform wrapped around his hand like a huge bandage. In another world it would have looked humorous.

*

At the disused Marconi warehouse, a few miles away, Boseman, Darville and Mendoza were starting to get anxious. The pretence of everything is fine was starting to wear thin.

Brad Darville was the first to complain once again: "When is our contact arriving, Larry? We need to get out of this dump."

Mendoza, the half-Mexican, lit another Lucky and smiled to himself.

Boseman said: "You know as well as I do, Brad. We can't move until we have the documents which incriminate the Colonel and us. Travis and Leo are watching the hotel to see who is coming and going."

Mendoza exhaled a cloud of pungent blue tobacco smoke: "It was a mistake for them to kill Brimblecombe without getting the material first. Cart before the horse."

"Yeah. Maybe," Boseman said, "but Travis and Leo will be here soon with an update."

"Let's hope it's a positive," said Darville.

QM

The port of Southampton, England.

THE QUEEN MARY was towed out of the port of New York by tugboats and commenced its Atlantic crossing to Southampton. She carried 979 crew and more than 1,600 passengers. Two of them were Colonel John Beckworth and his former military colleague, Lowell G. Saunders. The ship docked in the UK five days and 3,632 nautical miles later; not a record, but the voyage had given the two men time to conspire. There would be plenty to do once they had settled into Saunders's house at Chadwell St. Mary, near Tilbury docks. For the duration of the voyage, they remained in their first-class stateroom accommodation, apart from brief spells on deck to take air and exercise. Early morning and last thing at night became their on-board routine. And they did it separately and inconspicuously.

Beckworth's and Saunders's ID's and travel documents were all perfectly genuine: they didn't need to take risks. Planning for the voyage had been meticulous – they didn't want to leave a trail - and their families believed it was Army business. Their cabin had been paid for – in advance, in cash – to a travel agent in downtown NYC. The stewards and cabin staff would barely recall the two passengers who had eaten modestly in their room, tipped conservatively and never ordered any alcohol.

John Beckworth and Lowell G. Saunders strolled down the ship's gangway like innocent tourists. Once outside the port buildings and arrivals area, an anonymous black Ford saloon parked across the road flicked on its headlights in greeting. The two men smiled in acknowledgement: it was the signal they had been expecting.

They walked towards the car. As they approached, the driver's window slid down. The man's gloved hands gripped the wheel and he said simply:

"Chadwell St. Mary, Tilbury?"

"Correct," said Saunders. It was a password as well as their destination. The driver got out of the car, opened the rear doors and boot. The two men stowed their luggage and got into the rear of the car. No small talk. No chitchat. The minute-long loading procedure was wordless.

The driver was a man of few words. He was paid to be.

Downing

MI5, 58 St. James's Street, London, England.

THE THICK, ARMOUR-PLATED DOOR was firmly shut as it had been back in August 1943; the critical meeting with the PM, Commander Ian Fleming and Brimblecombe. This time three people had gathered in the opulent, sound-proofed office of Brigadier Sir Cyril Downing on the top floor of 'number 58' – Alistair, Freddie, and Joselyn.

Downing was more than just a high-ranking serving civil servant. Far more than a well-connected, highly political confidant of Brimblecombe. He was also a realist; a canny pragmatist who knew that sometimes, unconventional methods achieved great ends. Today he was in the company of people who had been forced to exploit such methods to survive. Alistair who had worked undercover in Nazi Germany as Admiral Canaris's chauffeur. Freddie who had couriered DAS SCHLOSS documents back to Britain and then, with Alistair, had prevented the Tabun gas attack on English soil; and Joselyn, who had defeated an armed Irish terrorist in cahoots with Heinrich Himmler in the same horrific conspiracy.

Today, Downing was sitting behind his desk in shirt sleeves, club tie, red braces, his hair slick and black. He laced his stubby fingers together and regarded his visitors as he narrated. They listened to him as he came to the end of his story. He had read from a detailed Police report, which included a death certificate and several black and white photographs. He sighed as he tossed the photos of Travis and Walker back onto the desk:

"So, there we have it. Mitchell Travis and Leo Walker are a pair of crooks – small-time villains – as my friends at Scotland Yard would call them." Downing accentuated the words 'small-time villains' in the voice he imagined reflected police vernacular. He picked up one of the photos and continued:

"Breaking and entering, contract theft, you name it. Very well known to officers in the East End. Regulars at the Salmon and Ball pub in Bethnal Green for fencing stolen goods. Leo coached a bit of boxing before the war. But, bizarrely, escaped National Service on medical grounds. Travis was a conscientious objector who passed the war as a fireman in Bow. They were never nicked and, frankly, I don't know why. Ducked under the radar, I suppose."

Downing paused and looked at Joselyn: "Does any of this mean anything to you, Joselyn?"

She pouted, vaguely irritated: "Not really. I guess 'nicked' means arrested by the police, right? And 'ducked under the radar' means they got away with it?"

"More or less, yes."

"They were cleverer than the police then?"

"Resourceful and lucky, yes." Downing continued: "But that's it."

Alistair sensed her mood and moved on: "Where are you holding them?"

"Cannon Street," Downing replied, snapping his braces with his thumbs. "Under Special Powers, we are not charging them yet under Official Secrets, because of the risk of exposing you three. But they will go to court charged with the manslaughter of P.C. Adams. In the meantime, we need more. That's why I asked you to come here."

"Poor bugger," said Freddie reflectively. And he meant it. Wrong place, wrong time. A few seconds either way and he wouldn't have been hit by the runaway car.

Alistair shook his head: "Miles Villiers is convinced Travis and Leo were staking out St. Ermin's Hotel, with real purpose. They weren't just there as small-time villains. The question is: why were they really there?"

Downing sat forward as if about to speculate, but then thought better of it.

"What does Villiers think?" Alistair asked, an idea taking

shape in his mind.

"That it is suspicious, of course," Downing replied. "The two of them had been sitting in that black Hillman – across the courtyard from the hotel – for more than two hours, according to the duty manager, Andrew Sullivan. He does occasional undercover work for Brim; observation and suchlike. And the clincher, those high-powered binoculars."

"So, they were waiting for someone?" put in Joselyn.

"Keeping vigil, more like," Alistair suggested. "There for a reason."

"For what, or whom?" Downing asked.

"Us," Alistair and Freddie said in unison. But Freddie continued: "Let's just think about this. Travis and Leo think Brim is dead, because they killed the man that they believed was Brim. Not Charles Wighton. Now they want to check on the fallout from that murder. Because they have been told to."

"Exactly," Alistair agreed. "They are keeping vigil at the hotel to see who comes and goes. As it turns out, it is us. Sally and Villiers they have seen. But who can they tell, now they are both under lock and key?" Alistair's mind raced. He had an idea

Freddie looked at his brother, but in a way, was addressing all of them: "Do we think Travis and Leo were at Caxton Hall the night of 'Brim's' speech and retirement party?"

"Not in the audience, I'd have remembered them," Joselyn

said firmly. "Maybe concealed or even disguised as waiters. And anyway, Villiers would have noted anyone whose face didn't fit."

"Only one way to find out," Alistair said, rising from his seat.

"Which is what?" Cyril Downing had a note of foreboding in his voice; an anxiety brought about by the brothers' unconventional reputation.

"Question them unofficially, outside the realms of your Special Powers and not in connection with the police investigation. Something entirely separate."

"Oh dear." The corners of Downing's mouth dropped. "Does this mean ...?"

Joselyn's sensuous lips parted; she smiled her magic: "Yeah, Sir Cyril. Looks like it does."

Freddie cleared his throat: "Any chance I could borrow those photos, Cyril?"

Downing raised his eyebrows: "I don't see why not ..." And passed them across to Freddie, who smiled wordlessly.

*

"Can you fetch the prisoner a Beecham's please, Officer Wilson. He's feeling queasy. Probably the lousy food you serve in this dump."

"Yes, sir. I'll go to the kitchen. Won't be long."

"Take your time, by all means."

Alistair and Leo were sitting in a basement cell at Cannon Street police station. And there was nothing wrong with Leo; the look of confusion which crossed his face was ignored by the departing officer.

Alistair: "A young nurse from St. Bartholomew's was robbed and murdered just outside Waterloo Station. I am sure you know where I mean, Leo. A taxi driver identified the pair of you at the scene." Alistair's tone was solemn, his words slow: "She was twenty-four years old. Her parents are devastated. She'd wanted to be a nurse since she was five."

Leo swallowed and tried to ignore the accusation. Was it possible – even conceivable – they'd killed the wrong girl? No, they had followed her. It was all bluff. He smiled. This man was trying to trick him, he'd have to be careful though. He sensed he could be trouble.

"Oh, and a man was murdered at a block of service apartments in Marylebone. It was just after he caught thieves robbing one of them. Again, you were both identified. This time by the woman in the apartment next door, she was putting her husband's shoes out for the concierge to collect. She saw you both, as clear as day."

Leo was sitting at a screwed-down metal table, wearing a white vest and trousers. The garment emphasised his muscular arms and thick neck. Alistair couldn't see the look on his face because he was facing away from him.

"Cat got your tongue, Leo?" Alistair's tone was matter-of-fact. He suddenly struck Leo from behind, across the shoulder with his balled fist. The blow was brutal. Its impact knocked Leo off his chair and sent him flying onto the concrete. Only his solid build prevented a major injury. Before Leo could move, Alistair stood on the back of his left hand, pinning him down.

"Brimblecombe was my uncle." Alistair ground his hand into the floor. "More like a father, if the truth be told."

"So what, I really don't ..."

Unexpectedly, Leo swivelled his powerful legs around in a half-circle and slammed into Alistair just above the ankles. Alistair was immediately swept off his feet with the force of the blow. He dropped. Leo was up on his feet in an instant, a boxer's stance. Ready. Alistair struggled up, shakily. Leo jabbed a left hook at his face. Missed. He followed with a powerful right to Alistair's jaw. He moved back to avoid it. Next Leo kicked out with his right foot at Alistair's groin. An inch short of its target.

Alistair was breathless, apparently waning. Leo was dazed from the fall, not sure where he was. A street fight somewhere? He had been in so many. He quickly composed himself and danced on both feet, hands at the ready. He grabbed Alistair's hair and lunged forward, driving his right elbow into Alistair's left rib cage. But not hard enough. He couldn't summon the power he needed to inflict the damage he must.

Alistair grabbed Leo's right hand and twisted it anti-clockwise until the wrist joint almost snapped. Leo howled in pain. He retched in agony.

"Is that how you killed her, Leo? Punctured her lung? She was just a kid."

Leo's eyes were wide with fear now. He tried to reply, but his lips quivered, he was suddenly freezing cold with shock. And sick. Leo cowered and fell against the wall, defeated. The cell door opened, and Wilson walked in with a sachet of Beecham's powder and a glass of water.

"Ah, thanks. He'll be needing that."

*

"Thought you were done for then," said Cyril Downing. They had watched the confrontation through a double mirror, the other side of the prison cell. It had also been recorded by a ciné camera; 16mm., the sort used by RAF reconnaissance aircraft.

Alistair, Freddie and Joselyn were now back at Downing's office at 58 St. James's Street. Downing still shocked at what they'd witnessed at Cannon Street. Even Joselyn was surprised to see Alistair so swiftly back on brutal form.

"Just a little play acting, Cyril," said Alistair. "And Leo didn't confess to anything. It might have been a waste of time."

Joselyn looked pale: "He didn't actually have to spell it out and confess. It's perfectly clear to me that they were Jessica's killers. And Charles Wighton's."

"It doesn't lead us to whoever issued the kill order on both Brim and Jessica Hope. I imagine if they are holed up somewhere waiting for them to show, they'll have to make a move," Downing said with an air of resignation.

"That's true, Sir Cyril. But I think we have moved forward with what Alistair achieved today. We know a little more about what makes Leo tick. He's nothing more than hired muscle. A killer." said Joselyn.

"Yes. We'll leave Travis to stew for a few days. I've got an idea about how to deal with him," Freddie said with an air of mystery.

The three of them rose to make their way back to the Ritz. As they were leaving Downing said:

"By the way, Freddie. Transport have delivered your wife to Heston Airport. She'll have boarded by now. The flight to Zürich is punctual. She'll be back with your daughter in no time."

"Thank you." Freddie impulsively looked at Joselyn, who desperately tried to hide what she was thinking. Another expression not missed by Alistair.

Salmon and Ball

Bethnal Green Road, London, England.

SALLY BROOKE COULD LOOK her most beguiling when she made the least effort to. Or so it appeared. With her hazel-green eyes, auburn hair and freckled complexion, she radiated health. She gazed at Freddie and made a joke about something – she always did – and he laughed. She took his hand and just for a moment the clock was turned back. Freddie knew he was on dangerous ground: Astrid was now back at Chalet Monte Rosa in Zermatt with Christina. He and Sally were alone, a frisson of familiarity and comfort between them. At least he could try and pretend it was all business.

They were sitting in the Salmon and Ball pub in the East End of London. It was six o'clock in the evening, busy with exhausted commuters emerging from the Tube station next door. There was plentiful evidence of the London Blitz all around, of relentless night-time bombing raids by the Luftwaffe in 1940/41. There were still bombed-out buildings, piled up bricks and rubble where people's homes had once stood. VE Day seemed a long time ago and the look on people's faces was far from victorious.

Freddie and Sally sipped half pints of IPA in the public bar, idly watching the clientele for signs of something out of place. The radio was playing BBC Light Programme, a dull music hall farce that was far from comedic. There were few other women in the bar, except for the barmaid Deirdre, an attractive girl in her late twenties and the surly landlady, Mavis. She resented the lewd comments of her male customers but encouraged Deirdre to sport her plunging neckline all the same. It was good for business.

The Off-Sales counter was busy selling bottles of brown ale, pickled eggs and the odd pack of black-market butter. No coupons were needed at that particular counter. And no questions were asked. The pub was well-known to British Intelligence and Brim's agents had had plenty of experience there with surveillance and duplicity. Today was no exception.

It was a little after six forty-five when a man dressed in a 1st Canadian Army uniform entered the bar. He removed his cap and glanced around as if looking for someone. He was carrying a dozen packs of American-made nylons, boxes of make-up and cartons of Lucky Strike. He moved toward the counter and Deirdre immediately recognised him, although there was no overt greeting. He plonked the goodies onto the counter and smiled. A good-looking man of about thirty, with straw coloured hair that had grown too long.

"Hi there, Deirdre. These are for you. A gift from the US of A," he said quietly. Freddie and Sally strained to listen ...

"What's the catch?" Deirdre said aloofly; Mavis moved in from the sidelines so she could hear what was going on between the handsome serviceman and her barmaid.

"No catch, honey. Give me a large whisky, please. Got any ice yet?"

Deirdre shook her head as if the idea was ridiculous, turned and dispensed a large measure from the optic into a tumbler. She placed the drink in front of the Canadian. He took a money clip out of his pocket and handed her a ten-shilling note, except he held on to it. She instinctively moved in closer to him to take the money and he whispered something. She said no and snapped the money out of his hand. He was clearly taken aback.

Freddie lowered his voice: "What was all that about?"

"Whatever it was, the landlady doesn't appear very pleased. Look." Sally pointed with her chin towards the bar.

The Canadian raised his hands in mock protest, sank his drink and ordered another. Mavis said something to both Deirdre and the man and he took out some more cash. More drinks and money were exchanged, and he ambled over to a seat by the window. Freddie and Sally watched the scene with interest. Freddie stood and wandered over to the bar and ordered two more halves of the watery pale ale from Deirdre.

"Friend of yours?" he asked with a charming smile. Deirdre said no as he handed her some loose silver. "Keep the change."

But Deirdre ignored the offer and placed Freddie's change on a beer-sodden mat beside the IPA pump. Freddie left it where it was and re-joined Sally at the table. A group of boisterous men came into the bar and suddenly the atmosphere changed. Deirdre was run off her feet with orders for bottles of brown ale, gin, whisky and packets of matches. When the noisy customers dispersed to the snooker room, they noticed the Canadian had gone.

A little later when it was quieter Freddie wandered back over to the bar. He took out one of Villiers's RAF Special Investigation Branch ID cards and presented it to Deirdre. The SIB/Cranwell name and Freddie's photo looked impressively authentic. She glanced at the card and then at Freddie:

"Am I in trouble?" There was a flirtatious tone to her question even though she could see Freddie had company.

"Not yet." He produced the photographs of Leo and Travis that Downing had lent him. "Recognise these two?"

"Yeah. They ain't been in for a while. Why?" Deirdre looked to her right, where Mavis stood and casually looked at her watch.

"When was the last time?" Freddie tucked the photos back into his jacket pocket.

"Dunno. A week?"

"Thanks." Freddie turned to leave but paused and pointed at the gifts: "That Canadian soldier who gave you this lot ... what's his name?"

"Larry ain't Canadian ..." Deirdre laughed a dirty laugh and wrinkled her nose at some audacious memory.

"Oh?"

"Nah ... American ... Alabama or some such place. I had to look for it in an atlas me brother 'ad for school."

"What's funny?" Freddie sounded nonchalant but sensed he might be onto something.

"Me and 'im 'ad a little fling a while back. But it came to nuthin. 'E's probably married, most of them are what try it on. Just want a bit on the side. But he gave me a bit of cash for my trouble. Nice enough bloke though."

"I see. Do you know where he's stationed?"

"If he told me I don't remember."

"Deirdre!" The landlady's voice bellowed from Off-Sales. "Customers! We ain't a bleedin' charity."

Freddie wandered back to the table and Sally looked at him with enquiring eyes: "Well?"

"We need to get back and see Alistair. And Downing, for that matter."

Sally stood and took Freddie's arm: "Pity."

*

Once outside, Freddie scanned Bethnal Green Road from left to right. There was no sign of Larry the American or of anyone else in uniform. Most of the military – from whatever country – had been demobbed at least a year before. Freddie thought it was more than curious that Larry, supposedly from Alabama, had been masquerading in a Canadian uniform. Was he trying to impress Deirdre with his appearance and lavish gifts? If so, why? Was it because he didn't want his real Regiment known?

They walked over to Bethnal Green Tube Station and he retained his vigilance. The drink at the Salmon and Ball had revealed some peculiarities.

Sally gripped his arm: "Thoughts, Freddie?"

"Plenty of them. Come on, I need a proper drink in the Ritz bar. I might be English, but I can't abide that dreadful drink they call beer ... do you think they sell schnapps?"

"Only one way to find out."

Baker

Cannon Street Police Station, London, England.

SERGEANT GUS BAKER was six foot four and built like a tank. In fact, 'Tank' had been his Army nickname, and nobody crossed him. With a mop of unruly ginger hair, he was both feared and admired in equal measure.

"In you go, my old china," said Baker, hurling Mitchell Travis into the cell. "You can join your old mate. I bet he's lonely. What was your name, son?" Baker's cockney accent was loaded with sarcasm.

"Leo Walker."

Travis was propelled into the cell with such force that he almost collapsed onto Leo: "What happened to you?"

"Some bastard nearly broke my wrist. One of those brothers. The one without the limp," said Walker. "I nearly had him though."

Baker cleared his throat to get their attention: "My orders are to keep you both here and let you stew for a few days."

"Do we get any grub?" asked Travis. "I'm starving."

"Yes and what about a solicitor? We need a brief," barked Leo.

"PC Tony Adams was a family friend," Baker announced with heartfelt emotion. "One of the best."

"Who?" asked Travis with a little more vehemence than intended. And then he realised: the copper they had mown down in the Hillman outside St. Ermin's Hotel. An accident.

"Dawned on you then has it, Mr. Travis ...?"

Travis looked at Leo, then at his feet as Baker continued his narrative, his tone raised for emphasis:

"The murder of a policeman in the course of duty. What do you think a solicitor can do for you, eh? A hotel manager and four independent witnesses saw what happened. Bloody reckless and irresponsible driving."

"Hardly independent," Travis said, unwisely. Baker could see he regretted making the blunt, stupid remark.

"Oh really? You can tell that to Tony Adams's grieving widow. And their two sons. One of them has polio and is confined to a wheelchair." Baker was struggling to control his temper; he turned and slammed the heavy cell door with such force the building shook. The two prisoners were left speechless. And intimidated.

*

Outside, in the dingy subterranean corridor, Alistair and Freddie were waiting. They had heard the conversation.

"Polio?" Freddie asked with concern.

"Nah, he ain't even married," Gus Baker announced with a smile. Travis and Leo had been taken in.

Alistair and Freddie shook their heads in amusement: they had bought the sob story too.

"Give 'em a few days locked up together in that cell and we'll see how bloody cocky the pair of them are then. One khazi, a Daily Mail to wipe your arse on and a single light on all the time." Baker smiled again.

"Is there a listening device available? We need to find out as much as possible about those two bloody villains?" Alistair asked and looked at Freddie.

Baker raised his bushy ginger eyebrows: "No, but there could be. There's a recorder in one of the interview rooms ..." He pondered for a moment ... "There's a couple of ventilation bricks at the top of the cell wall. We could rig up a microphone the other side. They'd never know. Good idea."

"See to it, Sergeant, will you?" Alistair asked.

"I suppose," Freddie said guardedly, "that given the circumstances, you can detain certain suspects indefinitely? I'm not familiar with the nuances of English law. But there could certainly be a question of treason and the Official Secrets Act."

Baker composed his response: "I'd prefer to leave that to your department, gentlemen. I'm not sure what department that actually is, but I know Brigadier Downing is involved so ..." He let his words trail a moment ... "But in my experience, they'll be ready to talk – confess – within forty-eight hours."

Alistair's face broke into a broad smile: "Are you thinking what I'm thinking, Freddie?" He clasped his arm around his brother's shoulder. Freddie flinched; sometimes Alistair didn't know his own strength.

"The Canadian soldier from Alabama, yes."

Alistair and Freddie turned simultaneously and left Baker with a bemused expression and a bunch of keys in his hand ready to lock the cell door.

"Keep them on ice, Sergeant," called out Alistair as they walked away. "We'll be back within twenty-four hours."

Fieldcraft

Bethnal Green Road, London, England.

JOSELYN WALKED CAUTIOUSLY down the road towards the Salmon and Ball pub. The person just ahead of her was a good-looking man of about thirty, with straw-coloured hair that had recently been cut. He was clean shaven and dressed in civilian clothes.

Joss and Sally had spent the entire day staking out the pub, Bethnal Green Tube station, Victoria Park and the busy junction at Cambridge Heath Road. At five-thirty they were both standing on the pavement under the railway bridge. Sally was attired in run-of-the-mill clothes, Joselyn the reverse. As risqué as she dared, given the time of day, the place and the envious stares of other women. She wore her wedding band and epitomised the affluent American tourist on vacation in London.

"That's him," Sally had suddenly said, "approaching the pub. Now. Quick. Go. Let's hope Villiers and Clitheroe are on the ball, eh?" Sally had handed her a crumpled London Street map, pre-war. Larry, as Deirdre the barmaid had named him, was nearly at the pub's entrance. Joss crossed the road and quickly caught up with him.

"Pardon me, sir. Can you help?" Joss didn't have to accentuate her Connecticut accent to gain his attention.

Larry swung around and was immediately enchanted by what he saw standing before him: a well-dressed lady with a shock of jet-black hair and piercing blue eyes. Her face broke into a smile that was at once magnificent, captivating and utterly joyous.

He was speechless but managed to summon: "Uh-huh."

"I'm lost. The cab driver dropped me at the wrong street ... I think." Joselyn held out the map so Larry could see the place of her destination ... "HJ Bliss and Sons, auctioneers are supposed to be at number 164. Right over there. They aren't. Here, take a look."

"You're American." Larry said, ignoring the proffered map. A statement.

"Sure. Why? ... Guess that's why I'm lost, right?" Joss brushed an imaginary speck from her cheek to distract him. "Very."

"So am I."

"What, lost?" She permitted herself a brief chuckle.

"No, American, Alabama." He was about to introduce himself

when he suddenly remembered why he and his colleagues were waiting around the pub: to find Travis and Leo for an update.

"Gee, I thought you were a local, sorry." Joselyn stopped in her tracks and made to turn away, unimpressed with the handsome man.

"Wait! Wait! Wait!" Larry called after her. "Us Americans should help each other out, right? How does that tune go ..."

She cut him off: "No, it's ok. You're in a hurry. I can see that." Joss looked at the old pub; radio music was emanating from the entrance. And laughter. "And I am keeping you."

Larry now had a choice: walk away or engage. His mind said the former, his body, the latter: "It's ok. Where are you trying to find? Maybe flag a cab and ask the driver. They have a wealth of knowledge."

Joss pointed at the street map: "Here. HJ Bliss, auctioneers ... number 164 ..."

She would never remember exactly what happened. An arm was suddenly around her neck, a pad soaked in chloroform was forced against her nose and mouth .... the feeling she was about to faint and then being caught. She was dragged into the road. And then nothing. It took around five seconds for them to capture her.

*

Out of sight, at the side of the park, Villiers had his binoculars focused on the distant encounter. He dashed over to Captain Clitheroe who was sitting in the Humber, a telescope trained on the same scenario.

"What just happened?" Villiers shouted, desperately.

"I don't know. One minute she was there ... next minute the Yank and the two other blokes were gone."

"Drive! Cut across the junction to the pub." Villiers got in – as the car took off - and there was a howl of protesting car horns as the Humber screeched across the road.

*

Sally darted out from her concealed spot towards the accelerating car. It skidded to a grinding halt right outside the pub, mounting the kerb. Villiers was out in a second, his eyes scanning three-sixty. Sally's face was full of dread.

"Did you see what happened?" Villiers yelled at her.

"No," she said defensively: "I saw exactly what you saw, different perspective." That statement was for the record, and she'd make sure Villiers remembered it.

"You were a damn sight nearer." Villiers was trying to aim blame.

But Sally wouldn't have it. She had to control her breath: "She was talking to Larry. Another man put his arm around her, and she was pulled into a van. You saw what happened."

"What sort of van?" Villiers's voice was raised.

"I don't know ... please don't shout at me ... a van ... double doors at the back."

*

Deirdre, the barmaid, came out of the pub and lit a cigarette, casually standing in the entrance. Sally ran over to her.

"Did you see what just happened?" Her question was loaded with anxiety.

"No."

Sally all but pleaded with her: "Do you remember me?"

"No."

"I was in here the other night with a man. He asked you about Larry, the American. You told my friend he was from Alabama. You had a fling with him ... he gave you gifts ... nylons, boxes of make-up and Lucky Strikes."

Deirdre took a pull on her cigarette and regarded Sally with distaste: "Oh yeah, bloke with a limp. You was sitting in the bar. He showed me some sort of ID."

Sally gasped in frustration: "Yes, yes, yes. Did you see what just happened?"

"No, I was behind the bar, working. What did happen?" Deirdre looked over Sally's shoulder at Clitheroe and Villiers, and the Humber, blocking the pavement.

"I think Larry just abducted my friend."

Deirdre flicked out the end of her cigarette with her fingers to save the rest: "Fucking Yanks." She turned and walked back into the pub without another word.

Sally turned and faced the others: "Somebody had better get back to the Ritz and tell Alistair. What's he going to think? I can't imagine."

Deal

Cannon Street Police Station, London, England.

SIMULTANEOUSLY, ALISTAIR AND FREDDIE walked into the police cell at Cannon Street accompanied by Sergeant Gus Baker. It was exactly twenty-four hours since their last visit. They found Mitchell Travis and Leo Walker both sitting cross-legged on the stone floor. It was grim, the air malodorous with the foul smell of sweat and excrement.

Alistair was first in: "Ready to talk?"

Travis: "We ain't 'ad nuthin' to eat or drink except bread and water. It's bleedin' Dickensian."

"You're being detained for murder," Alistair replied somewhat smugly. "And you could be here for another thirty years if we don't start getting some sensible answers."

"Such as?" Leo's white tee-shirt was brown with perspiration and filth. His muscular shoulders sagged.

"Who paid you to kill Jessica Hope? We know he's American.

We know you met him at the Salmon and Ball. Deirdre has identified you. What's his name? Who is he?"

"I don't know," Travis said and looked at Leo. "Nor does he."

"Yes, you do," Freddie said. "Don't waste our time today. We can come back in a month. Or so."

Then something crossed Leo's face as he considered – for a moment – the prospect of remaining in this cell for a month. And being back to square one. He looked at Baker who was standing by the cell door, keys in hand. And then the two brothers:

"Can we work something out?"

"Such as?" Alistair replied, his tone theatrically bored.

Travis stood up painfully and stretched, taking more time than he need have: "A deal."

"What sort of a deal?" Alistair said. "We don't have the discretion to offer a deal. You're prisoners."

"We ain't been charged yet."

"What sort of a deal?" Alistair, louder, but dismissive.

"We take you to where the Yanks are in hiding and we go free."

Freddie: "You don't know where they are hiding. You only met at the pub."

Leo also stood up, more athletically, to show them how tough he was: "Larry Boseman. US Army, deserter. I followed him back one night. He didn't see anything."

"You're bluffing," said Alistair, but he could see Leo wasn't. He was desperate. And so was Travis.

"They're in an old Marconi warehouse. Holed up. We can take you there."

"Not a chance. You'd just bolt as soon as we were out of Cannon Street." Alistair turned. It was all a question of timing. A game, in a sickly way.

Gus Baker – 'Tank' cleared his throat: "We could cuff 'em, sir. Take 'em in an unmarked police vehicle. They ain't going anywhere. Not while I'm around."

Alistair: "We'll have to get higher authority." He turned and headed for the cell door with Freddie. The meeting was over, apparently without a result.

"So, Mr. Valentine. Do we have a deal?" Leo's face was a picture of triumph; and it was everything Alistair could do to hide his alarm. But a trump card for Leo and he knew it.

*

Bishopsgate was quiet at that time of the afternoon, but as they turned in towards New Street and Petticoat Lane Market, there was more sign of life. The fruit and vegetable traders were busy piling up their horse-drawn carts with rubbish and the mouldy produce they couldn't sell. Food was still in short supply due to rationing. Once again Alistair and Freddie noticed the poverty and bomb damage all around them. It was a depressing sight.

The disused warehouse was at the bottom of Wentworth Street; a two-storey Victorian building that had too seen better days. Two unmarked Wolseley police cars pulled up outside it. In the first was a plain-clothes police driver with Alistair and Freddie in the back, armed and ready with police-issue guns. In the second car was another similarly attired driver, an armed detective from Cannon Street and Leo who was handcuffed to Sergeant Gus Baker on the back seat.

The drivers and detective remained in the vehicle. Alistair and Freddie entered the building cautiously, weapons drawn, Baker and Leo just behind them. There was no apparent sign of life.

"This is where they were," said Leo in a whisper, "I swear."

"Shut up," Alistair said sharply.

Alistair and Freddie scanned the entire downstairs of the building, listening, advancing silently forward, watching for tell-tale signs of an ambush.

"Not anymore," Freddie said. "God, it stinks in here." He nearly tripped over discarded empty tins of rationed corn beef, the remains of fish and chips wrapped in newspapers and empty beer bottles. On the other side of the warehouse were three makeshift camp beds and an old settee covered with dirty laundry. The place was rank: a pigsty. They walked stealthily, not sure what exactly they expected to find.

"Alistair! Over here, look," called Freddie in a hushed tone. "Empty cartons of Lucky Strike. And a few packs of nylons. Same as the ones Larry gave Deirdre in the pub. Larry and his associates were here. No question."

"Told you." said Leo.

"Shut up," Alistair said again. "Take him back to the car will you, Sergeant. He's starting to annoy me."

"Well, you didn't believe me, and I have proved you wrong. Travis and I want to go free. You said we could."

"No, I didn't. You killed Jessica Hope and our colleague. You aren't going anywhere. Get that into your head."

Leo huffed, knowing he had been tricked and there was no way out except prison. Or the gallows. Baker more or less dragged him out of the warehouse and onto the street.

"Cigarettes and stockings, but nothing else," Freddie said disappointedly. None of the pilfered Comms from Bletchley Park that Sally that had described to them. No evidence whatsoever. "What next then?" Freddie questioned almost to himself.

Alistair exhaled sharply through clenched teeth: "Back to the Ritz, I suppose. There's an outside chance Sally and Joselyn found this Larry Boseman, either in, or around the Salmon and Ball ..."

"And do you reckon Villiers was able to nab him?"

"Let's hope so, yes. We know for sure there are three of them out there somewhere, with the BP Comms equipment. We'll have to find them." Alistair re-holstered his weapon as did Freddie.

"We'll need to contact Brim." They walked out into the daylight towards the two parked Wolseley cars. "Yes, but with nothing to say except that our quarry has fled."

Hostage

Essex, England.

AT THIS MOMENT JOSELYN had no idea where she was or exactly what had happened to her. Her mind was a fuzz and she strained to think back. She was cooped up in the back of a moving vehicle, mouth dry and head pounding. She had been gagged, blindfolded, and tied up. No possible way of escape. Whoever the kidnappers were knew what they were doing.

All she could think of was that journey down to Southampton in the back of Devlin's car; the confrontation; the moment she'd pulled the trigger and killed him.

Suddenly the vehicle accelerated, as if now on a more major road. She could hear the men talking in the front; but the voices were muffled and drowned by engine noise. She swallowed, took breaths through her nose and forced herself to remember. What had happened outside the pub?

She had asked Larry – yes, that was the name Sally had told

her – about where the auction room was located. That was it, the fuzz was lifting. He'd told her he was an American from Alabama.

She'd held out the map for him to have a look at and then nothing.

Joss swallowed again and considered: who were these people and why had they risked abducting her in broad daylight?

There were other people beside Sally. But who? Not Alistair and Freddie, they were doing something else. She strained to remember but couldn't.

At some point the vehicle stopped, doors were opened, and she was dragged out. No words were spoken. Somebody wrapped the strap of her handbag around her neck, and she was pulled over uneven cobblestones, the heels of her shoes scuffing. She was led down steep stone steps – to a basement, she presumed – tied with rope to a chair and left. No light, no sound, no food or drink.

She was a prisoner, but whose?

Chadwell St. Mary

The Port of Tilbury, Essex, England.

LOWELL G. SAUNDERS'S HOUSE was in the Parish of Chadwell St. Mary, a stone's throw from the ancient port of Tilbury. It was a detached, self-contained Victorian property, maintained by anonymous gardeners which had miraculously escaped the ravages of the Luftwaffe.

Saunders's family had had money when they first lived there over a hundred years earlier. Their business interests were all to do with shipping, cargo and maritime transport. All that disappeared due to a frivolous lifestyle by Saunders's grandfather and then his father. They had squandered it on unwise business ventures, women, gambling, drinking, which resulted in an early death for both of them. Carbon copies. The one modicum of common sense between them was to put the Essex property in trust for Lowell G. so that he could not take possession of it until he was twenty-five. But, apart from the house, Saunders was broke, with no income, hence the criminal venture he was engaged upon. He couldn't afford for it to fail.

He and Colonel John Beckworth now sat in a second-storey bay window and quizzed Larry Boseman, who was perched on an uncomfortable kitchen chair, looking very pleased with himself.

"It's good to know all the Comms equipment is safely stowed, Larry. And good that you abducted that woman. How did it come about? Tell me." Beckworth's tone had an edge; he had gained an unforeseen advantage but didn't want to show what a useful bargaining chip Joselyn could be. Boseman might get ideas.

Boseman: "Yeah, well, we went to the Salmon and Ball to try and find Leo and Travis ... the two guys who killed Jessica ..."

"We know who they are, Larry. Go on."

"She turned up, they didn't."

"And?" Beckworth was not a man to waste time and Lowell G. clearly wanted to be somewhere else.

Boseman waited, watched the two: "She and another woman had been hanging around by the bar, the park and the road junction. Darville spotted them. They didn't look like hookers. The other woman – I wanna call her 'auburn hair' – was in the Salmon bar the other night. Sittin' with a guy I'd seen before someplace. Maybe St. Ermin's. Distinctive-looking guy with a limp. Looks ex-Forces."

"Ok. She may be useful," Beckworth said guardedly.

Boseman wanted to make his cleverness understood by both

men: "The two women – 'auburn hair' and the one tied up downstairs - are both connected to Brimblecombe."

Beckworth was unsure: "Tell me, Larry. There is no possibility that Brimblecombe could have survived, is there? Leo and Travis made sure, at that apartment."

"No, he's dead alright."

"As long as you are certain, Larry. One hundred per cent."

"Sure."

Beckworth walked round to where Larry was sitting. Larry wasn't sure what Beckworth was going to do next. He was unpredictable. Larry lowered his voice: "At least we know for sure Jessica Hope is dead because of the newspaper article. The London Times even had a picture of her, you told me so, right?"

"Uh-huh."

"But what Jessica stole from me – to blackmail me – is still very relevant and possibly damaging. The woman downstairs probably has access to it."

He thought about it: "Yes, she worked for Brimblecombe ... so yes, she does."

Beckworth snorted: "She'll deny it, of course."

Larry: "We'll make her tell the truth and get what you need."

Lowell G. piped up finally: "She's not leaving here until we get the money. She's your problem, Boseman."

Boseman smirked: "Give me ten minutes with her. I'll soon

make her talk."

Broken China

Gunfleet, Blakeney Quay, Norfolk, England.

BRIMBLECOMBE'S FACE WAS PALE, the telephone receiver almost slid out of his hand. He was standing in the window of 'the lookout room' at Gunfleet watching the bobbing boats at Pinchen's Creek and the sea in the distance. The sound he made was interspersed with sniffs, the brink of tears perhaps. He was utterly shocked.

Alice Trueblood came into the room with a tray of tea – Earl Grey for Brim – and dropped it when she saw his expression. She stepped over the broken china, teapot, strainer and a few biscuits. She grasped his arm. Brim shared his conversation with Alistair on the other end of the line in London and Alice beside him. He struggled for adequate words:

"It's Alistair. Bad news ... Joselyn has been abducted in broad daylight. East End. Salmon and Ball. Under the noses of Villiers and Clitheroe ..." The words came out like the china, broken ... "Yes, Miss Trueblood is right beside me now. Thank God ... no leads, understood."

Miss Trueblood had the discretion to know she must step back slightly from Brim's immediate personal space and released his arm. It was more than sensitivity and thoughtfulness; she knew just how much his close-knit circle meant to him. What must she do to help? She heard Brim say: I understand ... Yes, of course ... You have my full support. We will do everything in our power to find Joselyn and get her freed safely. Speak soon. It is reassuring for me to know that Freddie and Sally are with you. Look after each other. Goodbye for now, Alistair. Brim's words were shaky, and she could see he was very moved and yet remained positive to the last.

She knelt to attend to the broken china, and Brim was there immediately, down on his haunches:

"Let me help you, Alice. Gosh, pity about my tea. Here we are, pop it all back on the tray. The cosy has absorbed most of it."

"Brim?" She touched the top of his hand affectionately and their eyes met in a warm mutual understanding. She wanted so much for him to confide in her. He would reveal what he must.

"Alistair and Freddie want me back in London to take command. Sally too." He pursed his lips the way he did and chuckled, "In fact, Sally is the most insistent of them all."

"Will you go?" Alice at once regretted her words. "I mean when will you go?"

Brim stood up and stretched, wandered over to the 'lookout window.' "Tell me, Alice, is the M.Y. Gunfleet seaworthy, shipshape and Bristol fashion?"

Miss Trueblood, a mite confused, said: "Yes, she's down in Harwich. You know where she is. Near HMS Ganges."

"Crew?" Brim said, knowing it would rile Alice.

"I am her Captain, Brim. But there are some crew members I can call on. What do you have in mind?"

"That we return south by sea, as a precaution. We'll get a taxi from Blakeney down to Harwich. Can you muster local crew and speak to your contacts at Ganges?"

"Of course."

"Good. We'll leave first thing in the morning. I'll call Alistair, Freddie and Sally to put them in the picture. The game, as Mr. Holmes would say, is afoot."

*

Brim glanced over at the desk at the assorted documents he had studied and absorbed:

A US Pentagon Stores Requisition Memo, signed by Colonel John Beckworth, authorising Larry Boseman to take possession of the British Comms equipment.

A typed memorandum by Jessica Hope to the 'masterminds at Bletchley Park' – Dilly Knox, Alan Turing ....

The letter from John Beckworth (and the $200) to Jessica Hope threatening her with a Military Tribunal if she breathed a word of what she knew to the newspapers.

Miss Trueblood finished with the dustpan and brush sweeping up the broken china: "There," she said catching Brim's eye, looking at Jessica's evidence.

"Thoughts, Brim?"

"You know exactly what I'm thinking, Alice. You always do. Let's make some telephone calls."

Finally, she glanced out of 'the lookout window' at Blakeney Marshes: "Shall I brew some more tea, Brim?"

Brim raised his eyebrows: "Something stronger?" It was always the jokey question he shared with his cherished agent Lucy Fry, the heroine of Monkeypuzzle.

Alice smiled, immediately picking up: "Yes, why not?"

The Ritz

Piccadilly, London, England.

SALLY FOUND ALISTAIR AND FREDDIE in the bar of the hotel. Their mood was predictably sombre and there was no sign of Villiers or Clitheroe.

"Where have you been?" asked Alistair, his voice slightly antagonistic.

She was prepared for an even frostier reception: "Do you remember Thomas Trout at the Admiralty Citadel?"

"I certainly do," said Freddie. "Why?"

"He worked briefly with Commander Fleming, Naval Intelligence, codename: '17F'", Sally said as brightly as she could.

Freddie: "Trout worked in the Submarine Tracking Room at the Citadel. Nice fellow from Devon. Expert on tracking U-Boats. What's up, Sally?"

"We know that Colonel Beckworth is at the head of this Comms theft." Sally sat down at their table and smoothed her skirt down, ready for business.

"The man in the Pentagon," Alistair said, his voice was flat, his mind elsewhere.

"Yes. And we know that his subalterns – Boseman, Darville and Mendoza – are here in the UK, with the stolen Comms."

"Yes."

"You told me that these renegades had been hiding out at the old Marconi warehouse on Wentworth Street near Petticoat Lane ... but vanished. You went there." Sally said.

"Yes. What are you getting at, Sally?" asked Freddie.

"What am I getting at? Well, I thought it very likely Beckworth would come to the UK to claim his looted bounty. Oh, and to get the money from whomever."

"Wouldn't they take the machines to him in America?" Alistair sounded a little brighter and appeared to want to get involved with the speculation.

"Back to our friend Thomas Trout. Colonel John Beckworth and a Lowell G. Saunders arrived in Southampton on the Queen Mary twenty-four hours ago."

"How do you know?" Alistair was impressed.

"Ship's manifest. On my instruction, Thomas wired the Captain of the QM and got a list of passengers. First class state room accommodation. He is going to talk to all the stewards and cabin attendants to see if they remember anything ... but the point is, Beckworth is here in the UK!" She could hardly contain her excitement and her jollity was catching.

"That's good work, Sally," Alistair said, "I'm sorry ..."

But she cut him off with her wonderful smile: "You've enough on your plate. Did you manage to reach Brim?"

"Yes, we'll tell you in a minute." Alistair could see Freddie was reaching a logical conclusion based on what he already knew. He raised his hands gently to give himself time to think.

"Then it must be Boseman, Darville and Mendoza who grabbed Joselyn. It makes perfect sense. To take her to wherever Beckworth is hiding." Freddie's reasoning was catching on.

Alistair actually laughed: "They all believe – all of them – that Brim is dead. Murdered by Leo and Travis at the apartment."

"Aye, that was the idea."

"But what they haven't got is the evidence Jessica Hope gave Brim at Lyons' bloody Corner House. The evidence he has up at you-know-where." Alistair paused to catch breath and remember ...

"The fake US Pentagon Stores Requisition Memo; the letter she was going to send to the boffins at BP, and Beckworth's threatening letter to her."

Freddie: "Even if Beckworth manages to sell the Comms, there is a stack of evidence against him for treachery and theft.

Brim's testimony in a court case – if there is one – will nail him. He'll be charged with Jessica's murder too. He'll hang for it."

Sally sighed deeply and waited a moment: "So with that thought in mind – if they do have Joselyn – which they must – they won't harm her. She's too valuable."

Alistair clapped his hands: "Light at the end of the tunnel."

Sally: "We should order some tea to celebrate – Earl Grey? By the way, what's happening with Brim?"

Alistair and Freddie couldn't resist a smile: more secrets.

Captured

Chadwell St. Mary, Essex, England.

JOSELYN WAS NO STRANGER TO CAPTURE, but that didn't make her plight any more tolerable. Once she was thinking coherently, her first consideration was as always: evaluate the situation and weigh up the options of survival. She thought Alistair might conjecture she had allowed herself to be captured to be closer to the conflict. She had done it before, after all. But that wasn't true this time. She hadn't expected it. She had been taken by surprise. As she lay there in the dark, tightly bound, she replayed the moment – what she could recall of it – in detail: there was nothing she could have done to prevent what had happened. And it was over so quickly. Seconds, she thought. But what about Sally? Did they get her too? And what about Villiers and Clitheroe, they must have seen what happened. She remembered now.

The last time she had been incarcerated was equally traumatic. Her mind slipped back to boarding the SS Solveig at

Cuxhaven a few years back. She had been searching the cargo hold for weapons as the steam ship crossed the Deutsche Bucht. Then she had been challenged by Harald Wolf, lost her footing, and collapsed onto the tank top – steel deck – of the ship. Unconscious. She had come to and found herself imprisoned; confined in a dark cabin. She had thought of her Uncle Mark in Martha's Vineyard then – as she did now – and it was bizarrely comforting. She tried to smile under the gag which had been bound tightly across her mouth –

How many lives does this little pussy cat have?

It had become a joke because she had lost count. Uncle Mark. Yes, on Solveig she'd used her Swiss Army Knife. But where was it now? In her handbag. But where was that? She was strapped to a chair. Her arms were tied tightly across her torso, immovable. But her wrists and hands were free. Her legs were bound with rope around her knees and thighs. Worst of all, beside the gag, was the blindfold.

She twisted and rotated her body around on the chair trying to free herself, to loosen the rope which secured her. It was a struggle of moving her body around in tiny movements. But finally, after what seemed like hours, her fingers touched something familiar ... the leather strap of her handbag around her neck, but behind her. And that's where her knife was. Unless her captors had taken it. Inch by inch she tried to grip the strap and pull it nearer ...

Overdrive

Hotel Suite, The Ritz, London, England.

ALISTAIR REPLACED THE TELEPHONE receiver and turned to a weary-looking Freddie and Sally. They had returned from the bar to their suite; Alistair had an answer to Sally's question, after a lengthy conversation with their former boss.

"It seems Brim's caution has gone into overdrive. He is making the journey by sea from Harwich to the Thames Estuary area. Miss Trueblood is skippering the M. Y. Gunfleet." He went on to explain that as a seasoned sailor – and daughter of an Admiral – her seamanship skills were beyond question. She had sailed Gunfleet to Holland single-handed, as well as to the north coast of France. Most importantly, Brim didn't want the opposition to catch sight of him anywhere he might be around his normal London haunts. Caution was paramount.

Sally, still irked by the fiasco in East London, said caustically: "Villiers and Clitheroe?" Such was her contempt she didn't even add their first names.

"On their way to Liverpool Street Station to make their way to Harwich by train," said Alistair.

"Are you alright, Alistair?" Sally stood and crossed over to where he was standing by an ornate telephone table, under which was a pile of directories.

He attempted his charming smile, but it was a half-hearted effort: "No, but there is nothing we can do. The enemy have disappeared – we believe with Joss as hostage – from the warehouse and relocated to an unknown destination. Could be anywhere."

Sally returned to where she had been sitting and opened her folder full of notes: "Downing's men, on Brim's instruction have questioned taxi drivers and porters at Southampton. Nobody remembers seeing two male passengers whom we know are Colonel John Beckworth and Lowell G. Saunders. They didn't register and probably disembarked separately anyway, passed under the radar."

Alistair: "What are we missing? Leo and Travis have got us nowhere. The disused Marconi warehouse was a dead end ... What the hell are we missing?"

"Nothing," said Freddie. "We have missed nothing. All we can do is wait and hope ..."

Before he could finish his sentence, the telephone rang. A harsh bell tone that made Sally look up in shock; it sounded intrusive. Alistair marched over and picked up the receiver, silently praying that it was Joselyn ...

Barrow Deep

The North Sea, East coast of England.

GUNFLEET WAS WELL UNDER WAY, her bow cutting through the choppy sea at a brisk rate of knots. Alice was at the helm in the enclosed wheelhouse, glancing at the ship's compass. She was dressed in well-used oilskins as was Brim, standing at her side, looking out to sea. Laid out on the table was an Admiralty Chart on which were placed the traditional tools of the trade: parallel rules, pencils, and a set of ancient brass dividers. Perched precariously above the wheel were a pair of binoculars and her father's sextant.

"Do you know how long our voyage will be, Miss Trueblood?" asked Brim with mock formality. They were within earshot of Villiers and Clitheroe who were sitting behind them in the aft cabin. Villiers was engrossed, checking the battery connection of a Marconi SOE Type 3 radio set.

"Based on the destination you told me last evening, I would

say about six hours." She turned from the wheel and pointed at the chart with her chin. "I calculated that the distance is about fifty nautical miles from Harwich and at seven to nine knots with the flood tide, that's about right. Wind should hold, according to the forecast. But you can never be sure ...." She turned on the wiper which cleared a segment of screen from sea spray.

Brim took out his distinctive silver cigarette case, but a look of admonishment from Alice persuaded him to replace it: "Go on," he said with a smile. "You were about to say more."

"Barrow Deep is the channel we are heading for, and I've calculated the co-ordinates of our destination. We pass an interesting seamark on the way; and one I don't expect you'll ever have seen from sea level."

"Oh?"

"Knock John Tower. Built by the Admiralty ..."

"Ah yes," said Brim. "One of the Maunsell forts, built for defence against air attack and MTBs ... As you say, I've seen them from the air. But never up close as this will be. Very interesting, Alice."

"A feat of engineering my father used to say. Complete with gun decks and anti-aircraft cannons. Manned by a hundred men, round-the-clock during the war." She smiled at some distant memory.

Brim said: "Yes and I bet those towers surprised a few German pilots back in the day." He became unusually animated.

Alice joined in with a scenario familiar to them both: "Possibly even that tame Luftwaffe pilot of the Heinkel HE111, the one Alistair hitched a flight back on in '43?"

Brim laughed again: "Gosh, yes. The Gunners on Hengistbury Head shot him down; crashed into a field in Dorset! That was a night to remember. I can picture it now. I was at the Admiralty Citadel when Alistair's Mayday was received from a German aircraft ... it was very emotional ... even for a curmudgeon like me. Alistair escaping from Nazi Germany in one of their own aircraft!"

"He did make it back though, Brim. And safely. Alistair and Freddie saved the day. Caused DAS SCHLOSS to fail."

Brim was suddenly serious: "But not without Joselyn's contribution though, Alice. We must remember that. What she achieved was, well, quite extraordinary .... and brave."

They stood in companionable silence for a few minutes, both absorbed by their private recollections. How near Britain had come to disaster. After a while Brim looked across at Alice and wondered just how many such incidents they'd shared over the years. She was a loyal colleague: discreet and dependable. And evidently a competent helmsman.

He admired her concentration; for this was a side of her he had never seen: "I take it you've sailed this passage before, Alice? You obviously know the hazards?"

"Yes. The Thames Estuary sandbanks. We are already

threading our way through those banks at the moment. The channels between them are narrow and dangerous. Hazardous, as you say. And unmarked since the buoyage was removed at the beginning of the war. It's vital we get it right." She gestured at the windows. "Yes, I've sailed in this yacht many times with my father. She's named after one of those banks."

"Gunfleet, of course."

"Yes. The Admiral was given her by a grateful American who had ..."

"Fixed it!" said Villiers enthusiastically. "Battery terminal was loose. This radio set is now working perfectly. You will have secure communication with the Ritz. Alistair's call sign is Rhapsody; Gunfleet's is Harmony. What time are we making contact?"

Brim pulled up the sleeve of his oilskin and seemed to consider: "I'd leave it at least an hour. Even if things go according to my plan, timing will be tight."

Villiers agreed and glanced at Clitheroe. Neither of them had any idea what Brim's plan was, who was involved and what was the intention. Neither of them had needed reminding that Joselyn had been taken 'on their watch' and that no doubt some kind of rescue would be attempted by Brim's team. His orders had been patently clear when he'd instructed them to board the train at Liverpool Street for Harwich: "We'll need half a dozen thunder flashes, plus your usual weapons. This will turn nasty; I can feel it."

Telephone Call

Hotel Suite, The Ritz, London, England.

"MR. ALISTAIR VALENTINE?" The voice at the other end of the line sounded American, educated, authoritative.

"Yes." Alistair's tone was cautious. He glanced across at Freddie and Sally who were watching him with growing puzzlement.

"I am Alexander Duvall. Does my name mean anything to you?"

"No."

"I am the man who warned Colonel John Beckworth ..." He paused. "You know who he is?"

"Yes."

"Who warned Beckworth that PB of BI holds him not only responsible for Jessica Hope's murder but also for the theft of the machines. And I told him PB has evidence." The use of initials made the conversation arcane.

Alistair was taken aback by this sudden turn of events: "How do I know I can trust you? Such information is classified."

There was the hint of a chuckle: "Of course, you don't. But you will. Believe me."

"Why?"

"Because I know where Boseman, Darville and Mendoza are holding your wife." Duvall delivered the revelation slowly.

Alistair's mouth was dry with tension: "What?"

"Lowell G. Saunders's family have lived there for a hundred years. Beckworth is there too."

Alistair was shocked: "Who gave you this number, Mr. Duvall."

"Oh, I believe you can take a guess on that one, Mr. Valentine." His tone altered syntax: "Lounge bar. Ritz. Ten minutes. Bring the others too. I know they're there." The line went dead.

Frantically, Alistair tapped down on the switch plungers of the black bakelite telephone to summon help: "Operator! Operator! Where did that telephone call originate from?"

"One moment please, caller."

A pause that felt like a lifetime: "Come on! Come on! Come on!" Alistair had never sounded so urgent.

"Reception, sir. The house phone here at reception."

Joselyn

Wine cellar
Chadwell St. Mary, Essex, England.

JOSELYN SLICED THROUGH THE final few strands of rope from her thighs with the Swiss Army knife. She pulled off the gag and blindfold and stood up from the chair cautiously. She felt stiff, tired and uncoordinated. Whatever they had drugged her with outside the Salmon and Ball was still pulsing around her veins. She felt thirsty yet nauseous; she narrowed her eyes to try and acclimatise to the new form of darkness. It was pitch black. She stretched her arms out in front of her and immediately felt a wooden post of some sort. She slid her hand up and down a section of wood and explored further; it felt like some kind of framework or rack. A little further and the tips of her fingers caressed the contours of a bottle. A wine cellar: so, she was below ground. Almost instinctively she shivered and withdrew her hand from the cold surface of the glass.

She turned, took a few steps forward and advanced; her arms

outstretched like an acrobat, getting a feel for the space around her. If it was a cellar, there might be more steps. She thought of her training at Arisaig House at Lochaber, Scotland. The British Intelligence Training School had been brutal. But it had prepared her for moments like this. Captains William Fairburn and Eric Sykes had almost tortured her one day and she had sworn revenge on both of them. Now she silently blessed them.

What to do: explore your surroundings; smell, temperature, boundaries, threats. She squatted, her palms out in front of her and then crawled on her hands and knees until she found a wall. Cautiously she stood. There was no shelving or racking at this point. She leant back against the wall – cold stone – and inched sideways. Three, four, five, six steps and there was an obstruction. She looked down to her right and saw a strip of daylight no more than thirty inches across. Of course, it must be a door! She turned and felt for wood panels, some sort of familiarity, even a handle. There was nothing.

Suddenly the door flew open and there was a blinding flash of daylight, the shock of which nearly knocked her over. She yelled and squinted. The image was blurred but the voice was familiar: Larry Boseman.

"Now where the hell are you goin' my pretty girl? I haven't even started with you yet. My, but you look terrible ... you need a shower." Did he accentuate the southern drawl or was it real?

She swayed, trying to focus, the intrusion of the daylight

made her want to vomit. Instead, she fell into his arms and didn't even hear Boseman say: "And when you've had that, I have to ask you a few questions, and you're going to give me some straight answers."

She started to struggle, but his grip was tight and unrelenting.

He lifted up her chin: "I'm looking forward to this."

Duvall

Lounge Bar, the Ritz, London, England.

ALEXANDER DUVALL PERSONIFIED CHARISMA. At a little over six foot, he was well-groomed, with a classic square jaw, alert blue eyes and a face that exuded charm. He was about forty, his voice mellifluous, yet commanding. Obviously, a product of an Ivy League education.

He introduced himself as 'Head of Internal Security at the White House' and sat forward. They had found a quiet spot in the corner of the lounge bar and now Alistair, Freddie and Sally sat opposite him.

"Before we go any further, Mr. Duvall, you said you knew where my wife is. And do you have any identification?" Alistair was polite, yet anxious.

"Joselyn is being held at a place called Chadwell St. Mary near Tilbury Docks. Probably the port from where the deserters plan to escape. She is safe for the time being because Beckworth knows she has access to incriminating evidence which could nail him ... we'll just have to get there first."

Duvall produced White House ID, a passport-like document book with a gold American eagle embossed on the cover. He opened it to reveal his photograph, his name and DOB. The three of them inspected it carefully.

Alistair mellowed somewhat: "That's reassuring. Thank you."

"Not a problem, Mr. Valentine."

Alistair smiled: "And it was Professor Brimblecombe who gave you the number of our private line here at the Ritz. Our suite."

"Yes. The Professor has been talking with President Truman personally on this. How and in what capacity I will explain. I have to somehow contact the Professor in a little over an hour."

"How?" asked Freddie, intrigued. "Alistair said you were cautious on the GPO line."

"Ah yes, the inevitable initials." He pointed at the case on the table: "Is that what I think it is?" Duvall gave Alistair a knowing smile.

"I'm sure it is, yes. An SOE Type 3 radio set. All our units are tuned to the same frequency. Our call sign is Rhapsody."

"Good," said Duvall. "Communication will be essential."

Freddie: "What's the time scale?"

Any hint of levity which might have briefly existed between

him and Alistair vanished: “We will act tonight ...” He let the words hang in the air to get the maximum impact.

“... Yeah, tonight. And you three are core to the operation. As you know, Professor Brimblecombe is on his way by sea.” Duvall looked at his watch. “He will have moored somewhere on the Thames by now.”

“I apologise if I was brisk with you,” Alistair said. “Force of habit.”

“I admire a no-nonsense approach. I would have reacted the same if I were you.” He paused. “Now, are there any other questions about my credibility? If so, I have the President’s direct line at the Oval Office.” It was a quip, but they could see he was deadly serious.

Sally gave him her best smile: “Please fill in the blanks.”

“Thank you, ma’am. Right, where to start for perspective? We don’t have a Secret Service as you guys do. Not yet. But plans are being made. Currently the USA has the Federal Bureau of Investigation, founded in 1908. It deals with domestic matters. It is the principal law enforcement agency. I guess you heard of Prohibition, right?” The blue eyes sparkled.

Duvall’s audience nodded.

“You did have the Office of Strategic Services, though?” Freddie posed cautiously.

“Yeah, sure. That was a wartime Intelligence Agency which

ceased operation, I think, in September 1945. Coupla years back."

"Why are we here, Duvall? More's the point, why are you here?" Alistair's tone had an edge which Duvall acknowledged with the corners of his mouth turned down.

"Professor Brimblecombe contacted the office of President Truman the moment Jessica Hope handed him the documents which incriminated Beckworth." Duvall sat back as if that was suddenly all he was prepared to say.

Alistair: "Why? We haven't seen the Professor since he went into hiding."

"That's a reasonable question and one I will attempt to answer. The point is 6813th Signals Security Detachment is US Army."

"Seconded to Bletchley Park," put in Sally, keen to involve herself.

"Correct," agreed Duvall. "Quite apart from the theft of the Bletchley Comms, these soldiers are deserters. This deed alone is punishable by Court Martial, but we didn't want to involve a military court. Given the secrecy of BP, the President's Office thought Internal Security at the White House should handle it. With your Government's support."

"You mean President Truman," said Sally. "He thought you should handle it?"

"Correct again. I posed as a buyer of the Comms. But I have to get concrete evidence that Beckworth and Saunders are guilty before they can be indicted. Caught red-handed, as they say." Duvall leant under the table and produced an attaché case. He opened it discreetly and stacks of greenbacks stared at them. "Two hundred and fifty thousand bucks."

"Real ones?" asked Freddie. "They don't look it."

"Yup. Fresh out of the US Treasury and a clearing bank. The same old deal with no sequential numbers."

"Boseman still believes you're a genuine buyer?" Alistair wanted to get the facts clear.

"Oh, I think Boseman, Darville and Mendoza have a limited shelf life, as they say in the movies. Their job was to steal the Comms and deliver them to Beckworth and Saunders. I'd be surprised if they are still alive." Duvall replaced the attaché case and looked around to make sure again no one was within earshot.

Sally looked unsure: "So it was Beckworth who ordered Jessica's murder?"

"Ultimately, yes. Boseman found two hoods to carry out the deed. Plus, he had a very personal motive. These hoods ..."

"Travis and Walker." Sally confirmed.

Duvall puffed out his cheeks as if bored with the detail: "I guess they're the guys, yeah. Brigadier Cyril Downing has them, right. Cannon Street. But you guys know that, so I understand." He looked at Alistair. They had obviously spoken about Alistair's 'interview' with Leo and the outcome.

Duvall looked at his watch again: "It's time we moved. And don't forget the radio set please, Alistair. We need to contact the Professor, keep him up to speed."

"Where are we going?" Sally asked with a look of excitement.

"Tilbury." He picked up the attaché case and gave the three of them a smile they wouldn't forget. "Shall we?"

Operation Gunfleet

Chadwell St. Mary, Essex, England.

ELEVEN HUNDRED HOURS; BRIM, VILLIERS AND CLITHEROE were sitting on one side of a makeshift laboratory table, similar to a trestle. They were in an old Army bus which had been used as a mobile dental clinic and field hospital during the war. The windows had been blacked out; it was cramped but perfectly useable as a temporary headquarters. Miss Trueblood, it was decided, would remain in the motor yacht now moored near to Tilbury, on standby. Her Marconi Type 3 radio set would be at her side. She was flattered Brim had named the mission 'Operation Gunfleet.'

On the other side of the table were Alistair, Freddie and Sally, their mood apprehensive about the proposed assault. There was always a feeling of anxiety in such a scenario. But the overriding emotion was that of excitement, the primitive thrill of the chase. Duvall was sitting in a folding canvas chair which would have looked more appropriate outside a village cricket club.

Brim unfolded a square of paper like a road map. Once unfurled, it clearly depicted building plans of a house, including an architect's drawing of an elaborate extension to the rear. They all watched him carefully, fascinated.

"Mr. Duvall, once we had received Lowell G. Saunders's postal address, Miss Trueblood was able to procure this planning application from Essex County Council. It will be invaluable to us for carrying out an effective offensive. Knowledge of interior layout is crucial in the heat of the moment. We'll come to your individual roles soon."

"My pleasure, Professor," said Duvall formally.

Brim regarded his team: "The objective is clear. Rescue Joselyn, secure the Comms and arrest Beckworth and Saunders for conspiracy to kill Jessica Hope."

"In that order of priority?" Duvall quipped in an attempt to lighten the mood. It didn't work.

Brim: "Yes. Jessica was my niece. Why she came to me in the first place."

There was a collective gasp of shock and a five-second silence. Alistair and Freddie exchanged a quick, furtive glance. It was hard to know whether they were aware of this nugget of information or not. Sally certainly was. As a distant cousin of Brim's, she was familiar with the few family members.

“What about the three deserters?” asked Sally, her voice soft and flat, not betraying a hint of any prior knowledge.

Brim flattened the plans on the table and looked at them coldly: “Shoot on sight.”

Duvall did not have to acquiesce; his agreement was etched on his handsome features. Another expression none of them would forget. There was a sound of another vehicle approaching. Brim stood, opened the rear door of the bus to see a red Morris van appear. The driver took his hand off the steering wheel and signalled to him. Brim gestured accordingly.

“Ah, good,” said Brim. “I think it’s time now to discuss your individual roles. Alistair, I’d like you to command field operation, front. Villiers and Clitheroe know what to do, rear.”

Alistair smiled and said simply: “Brim.” He was ready for action. In his element.

*

Larry Boseman was leading Joselyn away from Saunders’s house, at the back, out of sight. His pistol aimed at her spine.

“There’s a black Ford in the lane at the bottom of the back garden over there. We get in and you drive. Is that clear?” Boseman’s tone was serious. He handed her the car keys.

“You’ll never get away with it because you’re too damn stupid, all of you.”

Boseman pushed the barrel into her spine: "Just go over to the car and get in. No tricks. How far is it to British Intelligence HQ? We need to move."

*

Villiers and Clitheroe left the bus first and ran to the rear of the house, ducking low, keeping out of sight. They ran towards the rear extension and back garden, mentally following the lines of the plans. Alistair and Freddie were next. They charged over to the red Morris van and climbed into the back. Sally observed with a stopwatch in her hand. She called over her shoulder to Brim:

"Four minutes."

"Good," he said simply. "They all know the plan. Driver too."

*

Darville and Mendoza were sitting in the house when they heard a sharp knock on the door. Darville went over to the window and pulled a dirty net curtain to one side. He saw the red Morris van with the ROYAL MAIL insignia painted on its side.

Mendoza was smoking a Lucky and reading the sports page of a local paper. He shouted: "That Duvall? About goddam time."

"No, it's a postman. Looks like he has a letter."

There was another knock and a man's voice said: "Post. Sign for. Probably a bill, it usually is!" The voice was jaunty and casual.

*

On the other side of the door, the uniformed postman stood, with his cap slightly back on his head. He was holding a letter, book and a pencil. He shouted for them to open the door; he hadn't got all day. To his left Freddie held a thunder flash and pulled the striker, a shortened fuse, four- second delay. He counted – four – three. To his right Alistair was ready, machine gun pointing at the door.

Darville opened the door and was taken by surprise. Freddie threw in the thunder flash, and it immediately exploded like a crackerjack, bouncing around inside the hallway. Crack! Crack! Crack! Then a concussive stun. Alistair was now in the door's aperture rattling off a spray of gunfire. A haze of bullets tore through Darville and Mendoza who didn't have a second to comprehend that they would die instantaneously. The hallway was full of smoke. And a smouldering Lucky Strike.

"Grenade?" shouted Freddie.

"No need. Two hostiles down. Terminated."

Duvall was suddenly there with an assault ladder and was halfway up it, gun in one hand, hammer in the other, ready to smash the window of the second storey.

*

Even at four hundred yards the sound of the thunder flash was loud and shocking. It was a distraction. And enough. Joselyn stopped dead in her tracks and turned. Boseman was confused and also turned, the gun sagged down in his hand. Two seconds. What could be happening? He didn't see the blade of the Swiss Army Knife until it tore across the side of his head and sliced his ear. He screamed, dropped the gun as Joselyn ran back towards the house, shouting for Alistair.

*

At the rear of the house, at the extension, Villiers and Clitheroe approached what looked to be normal French double doors, three-quarter-length glass.

"What do you reckon, Villiers?" said Clitheroe. "Shoulder it? Looks easy enough."

Villiers shook his head, leant forward and yanked the handle down, oblivious to what was on the other side: a length of wire attached to the firing pin of a grenade. The pin disengaged with a sharp click. There was a slight delay as Villiers kicked the door open and stepped in. The explosion was massive and instantaneous, throwing Clitheroe's and Villiers's bodies away from the house and out onto the terrace. They rolled lifeless onto the stone slabs.

Joselyn ran towards the rear garden, still shouting for Alistair. She could not believe what she'd witnessed: two burning bodies catapulted like dead puppets, hurled onto the ground. They were black and bleeding, spiked with copper wire and shrapnel. She put her hand to her mouth and ran to a walkway at the side of the house. At the front she saw the red Royal Mail van and a bewildered-looking postman. Alistair and Freddie were standing at the entrance, smoke billowing out of the front door ...

*

Alistair saw her: "Run to the bus, Joss. Don't stop. Keep down. Keep down!"

Brim was there and she immediately collapsed into him, panting frantically: "Who - who were they – at the - back?" She couldn't get the words out properly.

He clasped her shoulders: "Villiers and Clitheroe, I'm afraid."

"Oh, dear God, Brim. No."

Sally came out of the bus with a rug and wrapped it around her shoulders as Alistair and Freddie approached. Joselyn was shaking and fell into Alistair's arms. For the first time, after all they had been through together, she was clearly distressed.

"You're alright, Joss. I'm here, steady." He cuddled her

through the rug.

Freddie looked at Alistair, shocked at Joss's reaction.

*

"Hostiles!" shouted Duvall at the top of the assault ladder. He dropped the weapon and hammer, then stretched out his arms, gripped the struts of the frame and slid down, top to bottom in a matter of seconds. He kept close to the wall of the house – like a commando – and called to the others: "Anything?"

Alistair drew a line across his throat and pointed inside to indicate Darville and Mendoza were down.

Duvall was panting from the exertion of the drop, rubbing his hands. He called out: "Beckworth and Saunders are up there, but I didn't want to risk a lone assault; not sure what to expect.... what was that explosion ... after the thunder flashes downstairs?"

Brim walked over to him, oblivious to any danger: "Booby trap. Back door. Grenade or explosives. Villiers and Clitheroe are dead. Give me your gun, Duvall. We're going in."

Brim and Duvall heard Alistair, Freddie and Sally shouting their objection, but Brim was a man on a mission. He took Duvall's outstretched Smith and Wesson and walked into the smoking hallway of the house, gun cocked and ready.

Duvall shouted at Brim: "I'm right behind you. Be careful. They're probably armed. Couldn't see."

Alistair and Joselyn charged from the back door of the bus to the front door of the house. Brim and Duvall were already inside and out of sight in the swirling smoke.

A split second later, Joselyn ran into the house – through the hallway - and down the steps to the cellar, without saying a word to Alistair.

*

In the upstairs lounge, John Beckworth and Lowell G. Saunders were sitting in the same chairs as they had been earlier, looking very concerned about the noise and commotion downstairs and outside. Suddenly they saw a man, a dapper fellow, very well attired and clearly very angry.

"Which one of you bastards is Beckworth?" Brim yelled.

"Before you try any heroics, Professor Brimblecombe, Saunders here has his hand on a detonator which will blow the room and ..."

Alistair stormed into the room; his gun stretched out in front of him in a double grip. He immediately saw there was no detonator, holstered his weapon and handcuffed Saunders to the arm of the chair he was sitting in. Alistair turned to Beckworth and looked at Brim for guidance.

"It's alright, don't do anything rash. I need him alive," Brim said calmly.

Freddie and Sally came into the room and confronted the scene.

"It's over," said Brim. "We have our man. The man who killed my niece and stole our Comms machines from Bletchley."

Larry Boseman appeared from nowhere, the side of his head bleeding profusely: "It ain't over yet, Brimblecombe." He took a shot at Brim which caught him in the upper shoulder. Brim fell back against the wall.

In the confusion, nobody noticed Joselyn enter the room with the coil of rope she'd been tied up with in the cellar. She immediately hurled it – like a lasso – towards Boseman. He dropped the gun. The running noose looped over Boseman's head, and she tugged it sharply, so it became taut around his neck. She moved closer, wrapped the remaining rope around his upper torso and wrenched the knot tightly. He gulped loudly. Ten seconds and Boseman was now the prisoner.

She mimicked his southern accent: "I said you were too damn stupid, remember?"

Boseman was dumfounded, humiliated. He couldn't look at Saunders and Beckworth.

Brim clutched his wounded shoulder and said: "Get hold of Sergeant Wilson and tell him to drag this rabble out of here."

*

Back in the bus, Sally bound Brim's arm as best she could: "I think it's hospital for you, Brim. The Royal London are the most experienced for this sort of injury; it looks like a very nasty wound. I'll go with you."

Brim took hold of Sally's arm: "Before we do anything, I need you to telephone Brigadier Downing at MI5. I have to get a message to him urgently."

Sally was more than mystified: "Alright."

Brim continued: "Ask him to contact me at the hospital, wherever I end up being treated. It's vital."

"I understand. Give me his number and I'll call from a phone box on the way over to the hospital."

"Thank you. And give Alistair this discreetly." He handed her a piece of paper.

There was a sudden knock on the rear door of the bus and the postman looked in at the assembled group: "Professor Brimblecombe. I've called for backup. All three suspects secured, but your colleague did a pretty good job with the rope, I must say. Local police will be here in five minutes. Oh, and the Royal Mail depot will be wanting their van back."

Brim tried to stand, but was prevented by Sally: "Everybody, this is Sergeant David Wilson, Scotland Yard. Very well done, Wilson. Yes, take the van back."

Sally: “Right, let’s get you off to hospital. I’ll call for an ambulance when the police arrive.”

Brim nodded in obvious pain: “Don’t forget, Sally.”

Alistair: “What happened to Duvall? He must still be in the house ... I’ll go and check ... better secure that attaché case too. There’s a small fortune in it.”

They looked around the bus: no sign of the attaché case, or of Duvall.

Plan

The suite at the Ritz, London, England.

SALLY WALKED INTO THE suite looking flustered: "Brim is not the most tolerant patient. Royal London A&E want to keep him in for a few days' observation and he needs more blood. The bullet missed his collar bone, but there is extensive damage to his shoulder: muscle and tissue. Mr. Ratcliffe, the surgeon, told us he might need surgery."

Alistair, Freddie and Joselyn listened with concern. Alistair stood and went over to her:

"I'm sure he'll survive. Did Brim give you a piece of paper?"

"Aye, here." She handed it over.

Joselyn stood, wandered over to the drinks trolley and poured generous measures of whisky into four glasses: "We deserve this. Poor Brim."

Freddie took the crystal tumbler and had a cautious sip: "I had no idea Jessica Hope was Brim's niece. Did you, Sally?"

Sally poured some soda water into her drink to dilute it. She chuckled: "Too strong for me neat. Bad form for a Scot ... Yes, I did know, of course. Brim didn't want their relationship made public knowledge. Too personal."

Joselyn considered: "That was why he was so intent on finding her killer. In a way, it was as important as the Comms. And those two men – the actual killers – are behind bars?"

Alistair: "Travis and Leo, yes. Brigadier Downing says they will go to trial, but not yet. They haven't got a leg to stand on."

Sally touched Joselyn's arm affectionately: "I let you down, Joss. That day outside the Salmon and Ball, when Boseman nabbed you."

Joselyn's blue eyes sparkled: "No, you didn't. It happened so fast. Even Villiers and ..." She stopped, unable to continue. A few seconds: "Did that all really happen? God, after everything we've been through."

She thought of her Uncle Mark in Martha's Vineyard and the question he always asked: How many lives does this little pussy cat have?

Alistair crossed over to the telephone and unfolded the piece of paper Sally had given him. He picked up the receiver, dialled the hotel operator and gave her the long number, glancing at his watch to calculate the time difference. He had no idea exactly who he was calling, only that it was an American number. He'd no clue this was the heart of the US Federal Government, one of Brim's key contacts inside.

"Chief Justice's Office, White House. How may I help?" This was Fred M. Vinson's private secretary.

Alistair was cautious: "Yes, hello. I'm checking on the whereabouts of Alexander Duvall, please?"

Freddie, Sally and Joselyn were spellbound. There was a pause on the other end of the very crackly trans-Atlantic line.

The secretary was more wary than hesitant: "Who's calling, please?"

"My name is Alistair Valentine. I'm calling your office on behalf of Professor Nicholas Brimblecombe, British Intelligence. I have authority. The password is Troubadour."

"Ok."

"You can call me back if you're worried about security. I can give you our number at the Ritz hotel, London, England."

"That's ok, sir. Valentine and Troubadour is sufficient. One moment." Another pause, the hollow echo they had come to know.

Then a man: "London. Valentine. Troubadour."

"Correct," said Alistair. Freddie, Sally and Joselyn came nearer to where Alistair was standing.

"Alexander Duvall has not reported in for more than thirty-six hours. He should have contacted this office and his wife

Stella in DC. We're concerned he may have had an accident and is in hospital someplace. Maybe unconscious."

"No, I don't believe Duvall's had an accident," Alistair said knowingly. "I'm sure we'd have heard something by now, don't you?"

"Sure. Keep us posted." The American line went dead without further ado.

Alistair replaced the receiver. He thought of Duvall, the attaché case containing $250,000 and the Bletchley Park Comms. He wondered where they all were now. And possibly, so did Brim.

Alistair turned to Freddie, who merely nodded in unspoken agreement. Alistair picked up the phone again and re-dialled the hotel operator. He gave her a London number he knew of old. It was answered after two rings:

"Brigadier Sir Cyril Downing, please .... Yes, Alistair Valentine. He's expecting my call." There was a brief pause. "Ah, Cyril. Good evening. You've spoken to Brim, I assume?" Alistair listened intently. Freddie, Joselyn, and Sally watched him.

"Freddie and I will need to see Beckworth right away ... yes .... Is he being detained at your usual secure facility?"

Downing confirmed that he was.

"Right, we'll be there in however long it takes to go by taxi from Piccadilly to Twickenham. Oh, and we'll need him alone.

Get shot of Saunders, will you?"

Downing agreed.

"And tell the prison guard not to disturb us."

Again, there was verbal assent.

"Oh, one more thing. Is that Bell Air/Sea rescue helicopter still operational at Heston Airport? ... It is, good... Any chance you could get hold of an experienced pilot and have him fly it over to Twickenham? I've a feeling we're going to need a fast ride to Tilbury."

Downing chuckled at the other end and said: "You don't ask for much, do you?"

"Never."

Detention Centre

MI5 Secure Facility, Twickenham, England.

"I NEED A LAWYER," John Beckworth said without making eye contact with either Alistair or Freddie. The last word came out in a long extended southern drawl. It was more than two hours after the assault on Saunders's house in Essex.

"You'll need an extremely competent one, Beckworth." Alistair didn't need to spell it out. His tone was wry, mocking.

Beckworth was shackled: both wrists cuffed onto the tubular arms of a metal chair, bolted to the stone floor. His ankles chained onto its legs. He wore a one-piece prison suit: no buttons, belts, or zips. His wristwatch, ID tag and possessions had all been confiscated. The detention cell was windowless; beige-painted brick walls and a single lightbulb encased in a wire mesh holder fifteen feet above. The scene was stark and demoralising.

"I got rights," Beckworth said unconvincingly. He didn't even believe it himself.

Alistair ignored him: "Duvall climbed the assault ladder at Saunders's house armed with a hammer and a weapon. He didn't use either. Why? He merely slid down it like some circus act. His orders were to smash the window and kill you both ...., but he didn't." He paused to allow Beckworth to say something.

Freddie: "Duvall needed you alive to tell him where the cash and Comms were hidden. What were you hoping for, some kind of a deal?"

Beckworth said nothing, his jaw muscles clenching and relaxing, eyes fixed on the wall. His mind wandered: these people, though apparently calm, were dangerous.

"You planned to escape by boat," said Alistair confidently. "Where's it moored?"

There was a trace of alarm around the corners of Beckworth's eyes: How could they know the escape is by boat? That Chadwell St. Mary was so close to Tilbury Docks simply hadn't dawned on him until now.

Alistair again: "Our colleague is distressed that you ordered his niece's execution like that, in cold blood. And you must have once, what, loved her? You bedded her often enough, according to the correspondence she left ...

And she was pregnant. But you knew that, didn't you, Beckworth?" Alistair laughed cynically. "Your wife and daughters will be livid when they read your obituary in the newspapers down there on the Gulf Coast."

Beckworth remained silent, his eyes staring ahead, trying to ignore Alistair's goading.

"That's where you come from, isn't it?" Alistair slipped effortlessly into the Alabama accent: "I bet y'all cherish forgiveness down there, huh? At the church on Sunday mornings?" He paused: "And you organised that poor girl's murder, to protect yourself."

He stopped dead in his tracks, serious: "I don't see much regret on your face, Beckworth? None."

Freddie smiled; it was a convincing performance. Another flicker of alarm crossed Beckworth's eyes. Alistair wasn't finished:

"And Leo Walker and Mitchell Travis killed an innocent man, also under Boseman's instructions ... but, ultimately, they were your direct orders. Weren't they? Quite a list."

Beckworth was frozen, no secrets left.

"We don't – can't - forgive a list like that, Beckworth." He walked towards the shackled prisoner. And, with the back of his right hand, slapped him across the side of his face. The blow had such power that his neck twisted. But it didn't break.

Freddie took a notebook out of his jacket pocket, theatrically searching for a blank page and slid out a pencil: "Where is Duvall? Where is the escape boat moored, Beckworth?"

Beckworth was now shaking with fear, knowing there was more violence to come if he didn't tell them the location. His words were muffled, mouth leaking blood. One last effort: "I need a lawyer."

Alistair stood up straight, rubbing his grazed knuckles. "No," he said firmly and waited. "What you will need is surgery. And I'm not finished with you. Not yet." He turned to Freddie: "That was for Jessica, Beckworth."

The door's lock clicked; the cell door opened a fraction: "Everything alright in there?"

"Fine," said Freddie. "We're just getting an address. Won't be long." His tone was casual and jaunty.

Beckworth, his eyes dark and defeated, looked at Alistair and sensed something he couldn't fathom. He knew one thing for sure – he couldn't take any more punishment:

"It's Dock Number Four. A tall-masted yacht called Atlantic. Sailing at high tide. You'll have to move quickly."

Alistair's face cracked into its winning smile: Faster than you can imagine.

*

In the back of the car outside, Alistair slipped on the headphones of the Type 3 radio set they had brought from the Ritz and turned the control dial. Freddie watched him with fascination; Alistair had had a great deal of experience with radios and Morse transmitters whilst working undercover in Berlin during the war.

"Come in Harmony. Are you reading me? Rhapsody here." Alistair glanced at his brother with a smile: he knew exactly what he was thinking. They called it parallel minds.

Alice Trueblood answered after only a few moments: "Harmony receiving loud and clear. What's up?"

"Where are you?" Alistair asked anxiously.

In the wheelhouse of Gunfleet there was the rustle of Alice's Admiralty Chart: "I'm moored up at Gravesend Pier. So, I'm not that far from Tilbury, awaiting orders from Brim." She picked up her binoculars and scanned up and down the river, looking for any craft that looked out of place.

"Brim has been detained, Alice. Will explain when we see you ...."

"What do you mean, detained?" she said, cutting in, sensing trouble. "Is he alright?"

"He was shot while on operational duty. Don't worry, he'll live. Sally is taking good care of him. An ambulance took them to the Royal London. It was a shoulder wound ...."

"What do you want me to do?" Alistair could hear the concern in her voice, but she knew they were on a mission and time was pressing.

Alistair repeated the information Beckworth had given them.

Alice confirmed: "And she's a tall-masted yacht called Atlantic. I'll head there right away. Over and out."

Alistair and Freddie heard the sound of the Bell helicopter's engine at the same time. It lost height and hovered above the Twickenham Detention Centre facility at five hundred feet. They both waved their arms in the air; the pilot acknowledged and made his gradual descent into a field adjacent to the car park.

"Good old Cyril," Alistair said and watched the grass swirl as the rotor blades slowed down as the engine lost power and the machine settled. "I bet it will come out of Brim's budget, not his."

Estuary

River Thames, London, England.

GUNFLEET WAS NOW well under way and heading towards Tilbury, the twin 6-cylinder engines throbbed with power. Alice Trueblood stood at the wheel. Despite the lack of crew, she felt competent and totally in control of the situation. She cut the power – and drifted – something had caught her attention: the sound and sight of an Air/Sea rescue helicopter hovering to starboard.

Ahead, she could see the Atlantic – a fair-haired man was on deck – desperately trying to unfurl the sails. Her radio set squawked into life: "Come in Harmony. Are you reading me?"

Alice smiled and thought of Brim: "Yes Alistair, I most certainly am, and I don't think I have felt as elated as this since the height of the war. Better still, I can see the target!"

Brim

A week after the assault at Chadwell St. Mary
Winford Orthopaedic Hospital
Somerset, England.

BRIGADIER SIR CYRIL DOWNING opened the carriage door of the Paddington train and stepped down onto the platform at Bristol Temple Meads. It felt good to be back in the West Country, albeit only for a brief visit. When the inspector had clipped his ticket in London he'd said: "Welcome to God's Wonderful Railway, sir. Have a pleasant journey down to Bristol." The comment had made him chuckle and Downing wasn't a man given to sentimentality. It was early afternoon; he glanced at his watch; he didn't want to be late.

On the forecourt of the station, he took a taxi to Winford in the Chew Valley. Once out of the city and onto the A38, he savoured the lush green fields and rolling hills of Somerset. The scenery was beautiful and a far cry from the war-torn streets of post-war London.

Once inside the hospital, a Staff Nurse escorted him through a network of corridors and out into tranquil gardens. Brim was sitting in a wheelchair under an antiquated-looking parasol in an orchard-like setting. It was rural and idyllic, complete with birdsong.

"Visitor to see you, Professor," she said respectfully. "Would you like some tea? Your usual? And normal for your guest?"

"Thank you, Nurse Healey ... Cyril, do come and join me. Take those newspapers off the chair and chuck them down on the grass. I've read them." The nurse turned and left them to it. On the top of the pile, Downing noticed an airmail envelope from the United States, postmarked Washington DC. A get-well card from the President? It would be typical of Brim not even to mention such a gesture. He let it pass but couldn't help smiling.

Downing sat in the adjacent garden chair and looked at his friend: Brim's arm was in a sling, and he had lost weight. But, on the whole, he looked rested and remarkably well. The country air suited him; Winford had treated TB patients before the war and the garden felt peaceful. Ideal for convalescence.

"How's the shoulder, Brim?"

Brim pursed his lips and considered: "Mr. Ratcliffe, my esteemed surgeon, advises me I won't be fast bowling this season ... but not too bad. I'll need some physiotherapy, but the convalescence is re-charging the batteries. Thank you for making the journey down, Cyril. I gather you have some news concerning Alistair and Freddie? Operation Gunfleet?"

Downing nodded and looked around the gardens: "Why here, Brim? Lovely but remote. What's wrong with London?"

"Ratcliffe offered me Harley Street or Winford. Operates in both. Also, Somerset is my neck of the woods originally. And Jessica's parents live at Chew Magna. Been to see me a couple of times..." He paused, "still racked with grief, of course. It will take them a long time to recover. If they ever do ..." Brim paused reflectively: It would take him a long time too.

"Indeed. Tragic, Brim."

There were a few moments of silence, then Brim seemed to rally: "Anyway, yes. Tell me what happened on the Thames, Cyril. I'm itching to know."

"Well, your hunch was correct, Brim. Beckworth and Duvall were in cahoots, although we don't yet know from when. But we will, fear not."

Brim took out his silver cigarette case and lit a non-tipped Senior Service. Ironically, there were no smoking restrictions in this Parish and no Miss Trueblood to chastise him. His mind flashed back to the assault on Saunders's house at Chadwell St. Mary ...

The mission had been well executed and successful: apart from the tragedy of Villiers and Clitheroe, he thought bitterly. He had seen it all and remembered the scenario clearly, but something had not been right. He realised that Duvall had escaped not only with the stolen BP Comms equipment, but also with the attaché case containing two hundred and fifty thousand dollars of US Government money. Brim needed Alistair to telephone the White House to discover Duvall's whereabouts and confirm his suspicions. The Valentine/Troubadour codewords had been agreed with Fred Vinson's private secretary. His conjecture had been right: Duvall had not reported into the White House office for more than thirty-six hours. Or even contacted his wife, Stella in DC. The question had been why? It was all now blatantly obvious.

Nurse Healey arrived with a tea tray. Earl Grey for the professor, English breakfast for the Brigadier. There were some biscuits on a plate.

"Thank you, Nurse Healey. Most kind." Brim smiled. She glimpsed the airmail envelope from America – she had never seen such a thing – and withdrew respectfully.

Downing cleared his throat: "As you requested, Alistair and Freddie went to the detention centre in Twickenham. They managed to persuade Beckworth to tell them whereabouts at Tilbury Dock the escape boat was moored."

"Alistair can be persuasive."

Downing continued: "Alistair and Freddie recovered all the stolen Comms from Bletchley and the attaché case full of dollars. Catching Duvall red-handed was the icing. Miss Trueblood brought up the rear and it was she who handed Duvall over to the Thames River Police."

Brim smiled: "Good old Alice. Excellent." He poured his tea awkwardly and bade his visitor do the same. No milk or sugar made his exercise simpler. He continued his line of reasoning out loud, so Downing could share it:

"Yes. You see there must have been a few moments when Beckworth and Duvall were left alone in the house, but I'm damned if I can remember exactly when. Possibly when Alistair left the bus and went off to try and find Duvall. They were all fussing over me and deeply upset about Villiers and Clitheroe."

"Duvall must have got away from the house pretty damn quickly?" asked Downing, pouring his tea and munching one of Nurse Healey's biscuits. "I wonder how?"

Brim sighed and peered up at the cloudless sky: "I've been thinking about that. No, I think he must have concealed himself somewhere in the garden or house. Not the wine cellar, because Joselyn would have seen him when she went down there and grabbed the rope ... Good God, you should have seen her in action with that lasso ... such incredible skill. It was like something out of the wild west. Her uncle Mark in Massachusetts taught her well."

"She's quite a girl, Brim. All your spies have such enviable panache!"

Brim enjoyed the compliment: "They certainly do." He paused a moment. "Oh, and the 'postman' swears he didn't see anyone leave the house. I've read his statement. And surely, he'd have mentioned it at the time? No, Duvall was resourceful. He took a risk, but then, he had a great deal at stake, didn't he?"

Downing huffed disinterest: "He'll get what he deserves and so will Beckworth. In the end that's all that matters."

Brim agreed: "You'll make a full report to the White House, Cyril?" He stubbed out his cigarette, finished his tea. "I suppose we'll have to repatriate them to the United States, although part of me believes they should both be tried in a British court, particularly Beckworth. Out of my hands now, thank goodness. It's political."

"Yes, and complicated. MI5 won't contest repatriation; the Americans can have them as far as we're concerned. And don't worry, my secretary is typing up my report as we speak. I re-read my draft on the train down here from Paddington."

"Let me cast my eye over it before it goes, will you?"

"Of course, Brim." Downing stood, sensing the meeting had reached its natural conclusion: "What's next on the agenda then, other than taking it easy for a while."

Brim stood up from the wheelchair to shake Downing's hand: "Alistair, Joselyn, Freddie and Sally are travelling down to Bristol tomorrow. Staying at the Grand Spa Hotel. That's the one with the fabulous views of the Clifton Suspension Bridge."

"The Brimblecombe team did a fine job, Brim. I'd love to have seen Duvall's face when he finally got nabbed by Alistair and Freddie."

Brim pursed his lips the way he did: "So would I. But I'm sure they'll give me a detailed recount over gin and tonics at the Spa tomorrow."

Downing laughed and then became serious: "Are you still certain about retiring?" The two men strolled up towards the hospital and Downing's waiting taxi.

"Afraid so, yes. Tomorrow will be the last time we all meet. Officially, at least."

"You'll be missed, of course ... the corridors of Whitehall will be as dull as ditch water without you, Brim."

Brim suddenly turned to Downing: "Do you know what occurred to me while I lay back there daydreaming the other day, Cyril?"

Downing looked at Brim deadpan: "Where you put your secateurs?"

Brim ignored him: "Why didn't someone at GC&CS slap a patent on all the intellectual property they had developed at Bletchley? The Comms we've been chasing?"

Downing frowned, a notion unconsidered, as Brim continued:

"We now know BP broke into Nazi Germany's most formidable cypher machine ... And broke it. Astonishing. They eavesdropped on the Reich's High Command and even Hitler himself! Not to mention the Japanese signals Jessica was working on."

"And?"

"Why didn't they protect it? One day, I am sure this 'computer' technology will have immense commercial value. The truth will out in the end, I am sure."

But Downing was doubtful: "I can't really see why, Brim. Who would have a practical use for such technology?"

Brim shook his head with a hint of exasperation as they approached the back entrance to the hospital. Downing asked one final question:

"Are you sure you can't be persuaded to change your mind, Brim?" Downing turned away with a final gesture of farewell.

"No." Brim felt a wave of sadness, the thought of computers and patents now banished to the back of his mind. All he could think of was the terrible fate of Jessica Hope, of Villiers and Clitheroe. It was the end of an era, his swansong.

As he turned to go back to his wheelchair, he saw a figure standing alone in the garden. For a split second he was convinced it was Jessica: the same composure, the same grace and assurance. She was wearing a long summer dress and shielding her eyes from the sun with her hand. Then she spotted him and moved slowly towards him. She took his breath away as she came closer ...

Lucy Fry was full of surprises: still striking to look at: long dark auburn hair, a symmetrical face, blue eyes, and high cheekbones:

"Hello, Brim. Freddie told me you'd been in the wars. Now I can see he was serious. What on earth have you been up to?"

She took his hand and kissed him affectionately on both cheeks.

"Lucy! You have absolutely brightened up my day. Cup of tea?"

She gave him that wonderful smile and raised her eyebrows the way he always did:

"Something stronger?"

Brim smiled, immediately picking up: "Yes, Lucy. Why not?"

THE END

Notes from the Author

Conducting research for the Valentine Series has involved a great deal of reading. 'One of my bibles out here' to quote Ian Fleming was 'Colossus – Bletchley Park's greatest secret,' by Paul Cannon. This lengthy tome was a treasure trove of information.

A few years back, I posed a couple of speculative questions to one of the (BP) curators: "What happened to all of those machines at BP after the war? And secondly: "What if a few had been purloined and developed by unscrupulous Americans – or whoever?

He referred me to the above book and many others, and I thought this story would make a great final adventure for Brim and his team. This sequence, in particular, fascinated me. And why I chose to use an element of this in the scene with Brim and Downing, in the garden at Winford Hospital:

"This story (of who invented modern computers) is not just another example of how the US computer industry and its offshoots have pushed to the fore, establishing the computer and now the internet as quintessentially American technologies, even in the areas where Britain was once in the forefront, such as cryptography. In fact, the story is almost a re-run of the Colossus story in one significant aspect. For, in fact, an automated key system, identical in all essential points to the DIFFIE-HELLMAN and RSA solution, had already been developed in secret in Britain at GCHQ some years before it was re-invented in the public sector in the USA.

In the late 1960s and early 1970s James Ellis, Clifford Cox and Malcolm Williamson, between them, had become the real inventors of public key cryptography. But they had not applied for a patent, not even when the software engineers in the USA started making their own patent applications, and the concept irretrievably entered the public domain. Indeed, it was only in the late 1990s that GCHQ announced that it had indeed beaten DIFFIE-HELLMAN and RSA to the mark. Williamson later reported that he had 'tried to get (GCHQ) to block the US patent. We could have done that, but in fact people higher up didn't want us to. Patents are complicated ... The advice we received was 'don't bother.' Cox recalled that you 'accept that (when you work for GCHQ). Internal recognition is all you get.'" (1) See Bibliography for reference.

Background to Jessica Hope

At 18 years of age Charlotte Vine-Stevens left college in Shropshire and volunteered for the ATS, the Women's Army. After basic training she was given a travel warrant and instructions to report to Bletchley Station. Her abilities had already been recognised by those in authority.

Between 1941 and 1945 Charlotte found herself stationed at the Government Code & Cypher School's codebreaking operation at Bletchley Park.

After working with Major Ralph Tester in the mansion, she moved to the Japanese Section in Block F to paraphrase deciphered Japanese messages. In 1945 this work led Charlotte to see out the war in the Pacific at the Pentagon. Jessica Hope's character is based upon Charlotte and other ATS girls at the time.

Bibliography

'Bletchley Park and D-Day.'

David Kenyon. Yale University Press. 2019.

ISBN 978-0-300-24357-4

'The Debs of Bletchley Park.'

Michael Smith. Aurum Press Ltd. 2015

ISBN 978-1-78131-388-6

'Enigma – the battle for the code.'

Hugh Sebag-Montefiore. Weidenfeld & Nicholson 2000.

ISBN 0-297-84251-X

'Colossus – Bletchley Park's greatest secret.'

Paul Gannon. Atlantic Books 2006.

ISBN 9-781843-543312

'Secret Postings – Bletchley Park to the Pentagon.'

Charlotte Webb. Book Tower Publishing 2011.

ISBN 978-09557-16478

'The secret life of Bletchley Park.'

Sinclair McKay. Aurum Press Ltd. 2011.

ISBN 978—1-84513-633-8

1. S Levy, Crypto: Secrecy and Privacy in the New Code War, London 2000, 325-8.

Thank You:

My wife Pam for putting up with me during the lengthy process of writing, re-writing, and editing this manuscript. And to Marianne, always my first reader.

David Kenyon, Research Historian, Bletchley Park Trust.

Martin Garside, Port of London Authority.

Deb Schoman, Matthews Boat Owner Association.

Iain Healey, Former Avon and Somerset Police Officer.

Rebecca Hopfinger, Antique Boat Museum, Clayton, New York.

Richard Daley, Blakeney Area Historical Society.

Tony Prosser, my oldest friend, best man and former Merchant Navy Officer.

Henry Rogers, WA7YBS, Radio Boulevard, USA.

Charles Penfold, thank you for all the nautical advice on Barrow Deep.

To JP for such a great edit and for providing so many creative suggestions.

Len Greenwood for the original artwork and continued enthusiasm for the Valentine Series

Stuart Amesbury for his meticulous research and feedback.

I would also like to mention again and thank Sally Brimblecombe for permitting me to use her late husband's name. Nick was a great friend, but never known as 'Brim'. That was purely invented for the Valentine Series.

And finally, to my two wonderful sons, James and Nibby, who have made me enormously proud. A man could not wish for a finer family. I am blessed with such good fortune.

Robert Wallace

May 2023

List of Characters and Organisations

Jessica Hope, Bletchley Park cryptographer

Professor Nicholas Brimblecombe, head of British Intelligence

Alistair Valentine, Rretired agent

Joselyn Retired, Agent, wife of Alistair

Freddie Valentine, Retired agent

Astrid, retired agent, Wife of Freddie

Sally Brooke, Former nurse

Colonel John Beckworth, The Pentagon

Alice Trueblood, Brim's secretary, retired

Grp Capt. Miles Villiers, RAF Special Investigations

Larry Boseman, 6813th US Army / deserter

Brad Darville, 6813th US Army / deserter

Mendoza, 6813th US Army / deserter

Captain Clitheroe, Brimblecombe's driver

Leo Walker, Hired killer

Mitchell Travis, Leo Walker's partner

Lowell G. Saunders, Beckworth's associate

Brigadier Sir Cyril Downing, MI5

Lucy, barmaid Salmon and Ball

Sergeant Gus Baker, Cannon St. Police Station

Alexander Duvall, White House internal security

Sergeant David Wilson, Scotland Yard / ‘postman’.

Lucy Fry, Retired spy / Monkeypuzzle

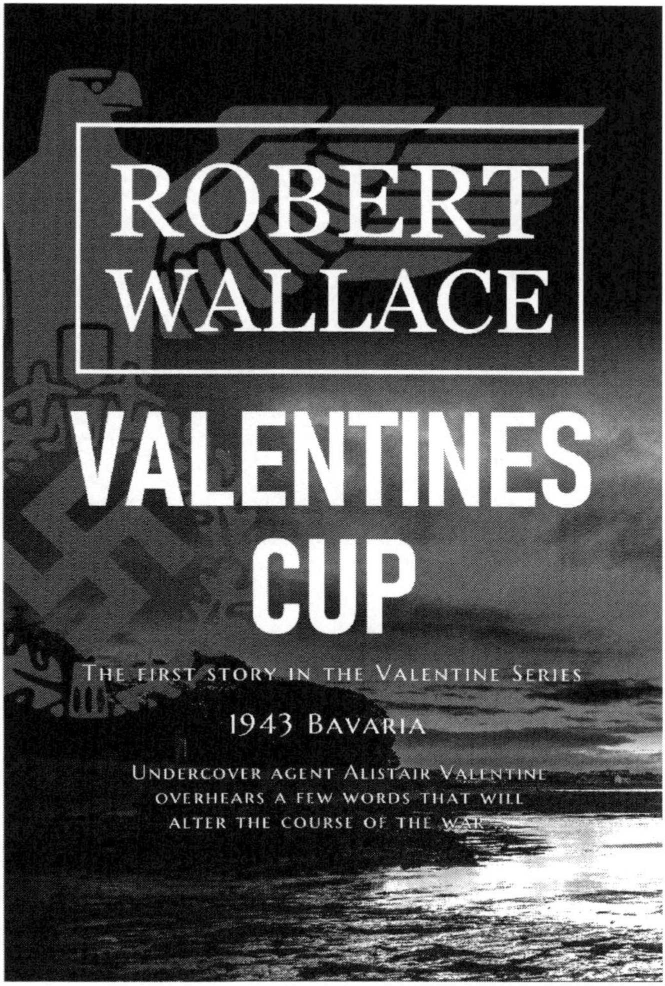
ROBERT
WALLACE
VALENTINES
CUP
THE FIRST STORY IN THE VALENTINE SERIES
1943 BAVARIA
UNDERCOVER AGENT ALISTAIR VALENTINE
OVERHEARS A FEW WORDS THAT WILL
ALTER THE COURSE OF THE WAR...

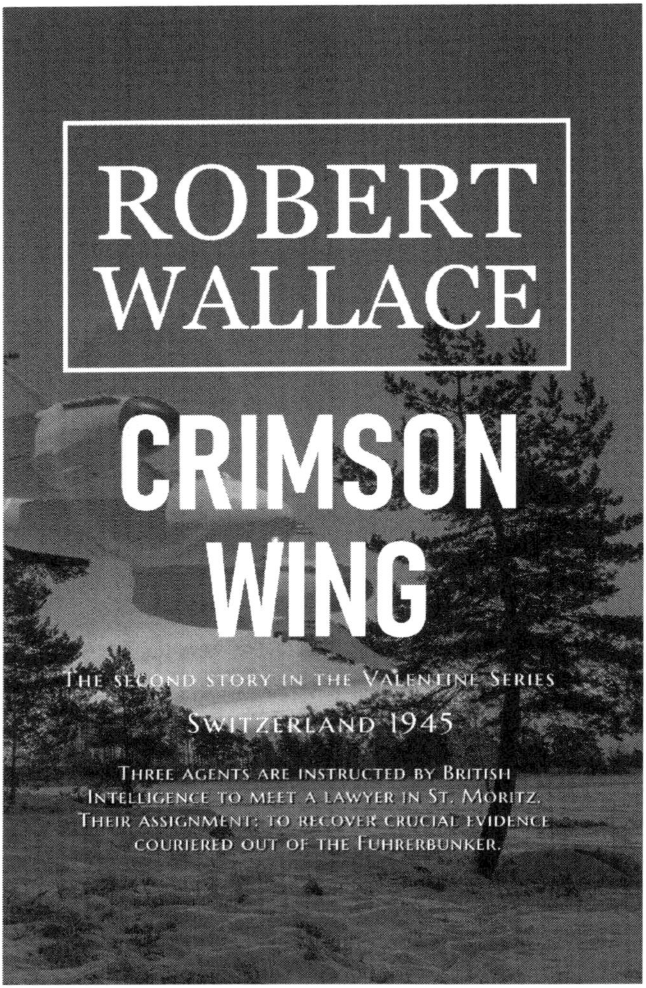
ROBERT
WALLACE
CRIMSON
WING
The second story in the Valentine Series
Switzerland 1945
Three agents are instructed by British Intelligence to meet a lawyer in St. Moritz. Their assignment: to recover crucial evidence couriered out of the Fuhrerbunker.

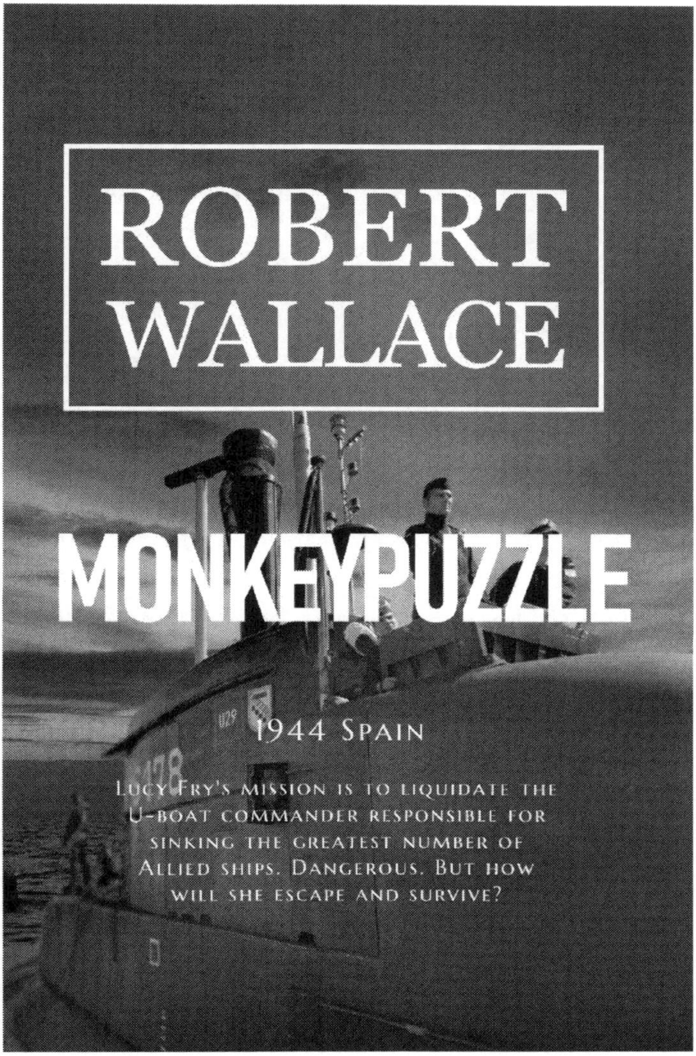
ROBERT
WALLACE
MONKEYPUZZLE
1944 SPAIN
LUCY FRY'S MISSION IS TO LIQUIDATE THE U-BOAT COMMANDER RESPONSIBLE FOR SINKING THE GREATEST NUMBER OF ALLIED SHIPS. DANGEROUS. BUT HOW WILL SHE ESCAPE AND SURVIVE?

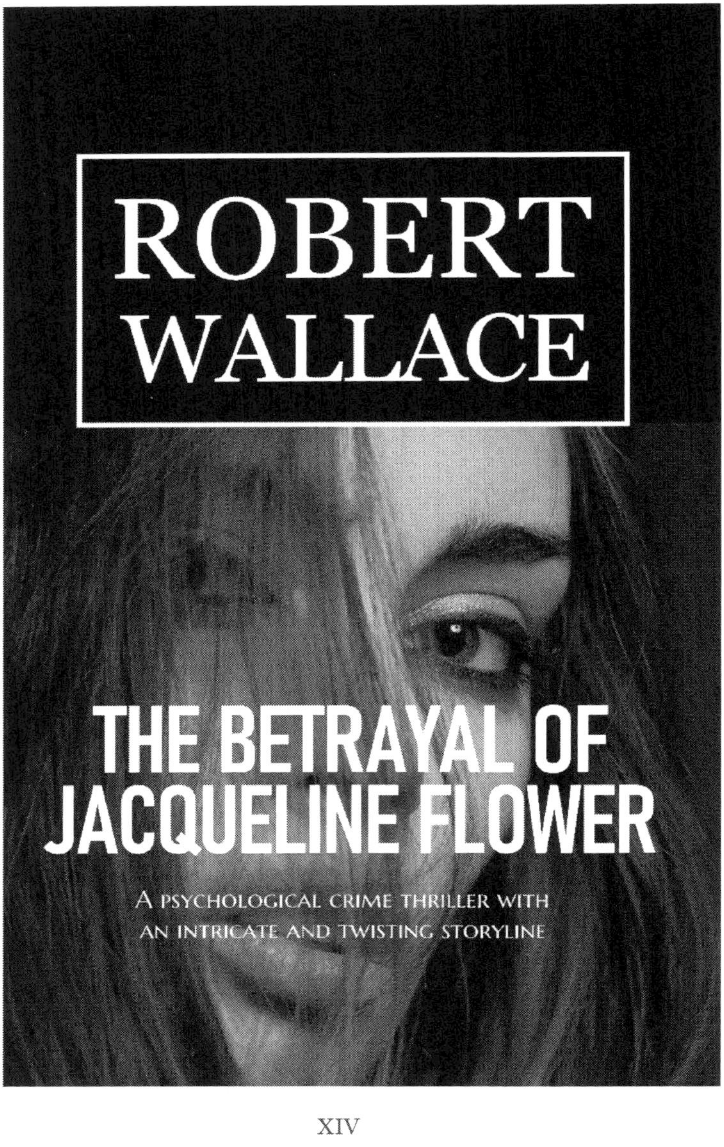
ROBERT
WALLACE
THE BETRAYAL OF
JACQUELINE FLOWER
A psychological crime thriller with
an intricate and twisting storyline

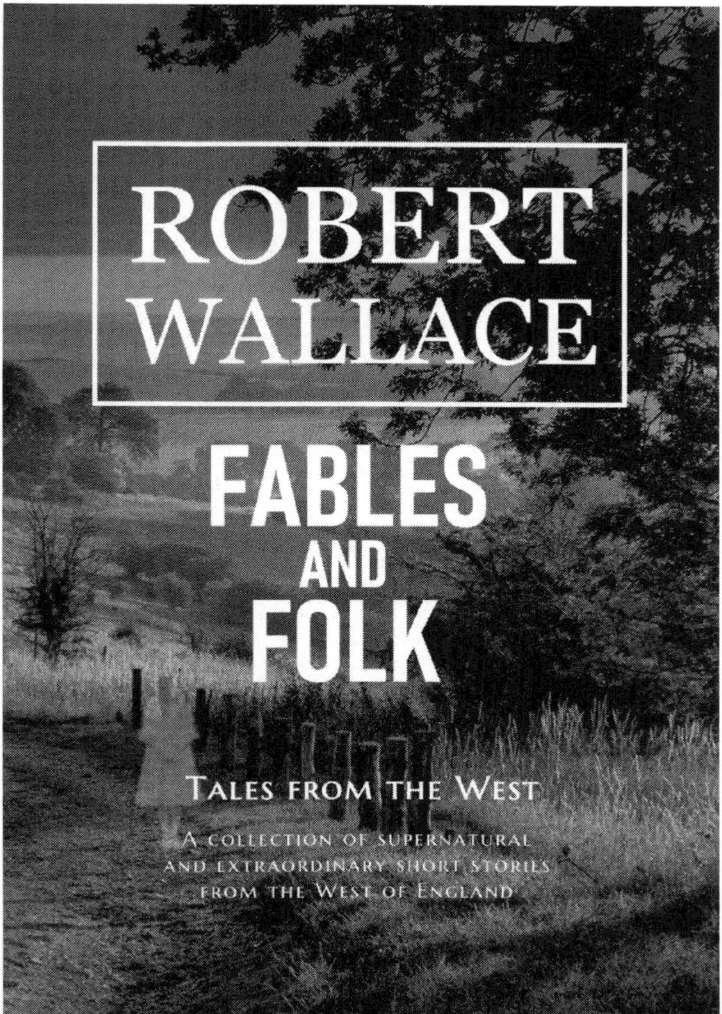
ROBERT
WALLACE
FABLES
AND
FOLK
TALES FROM THE WEST
A COLLECTION OF SUPERNATURAL
AND EXTRAORDINARY SHORT STORIES
FROM THE WEST OF ENGLAND

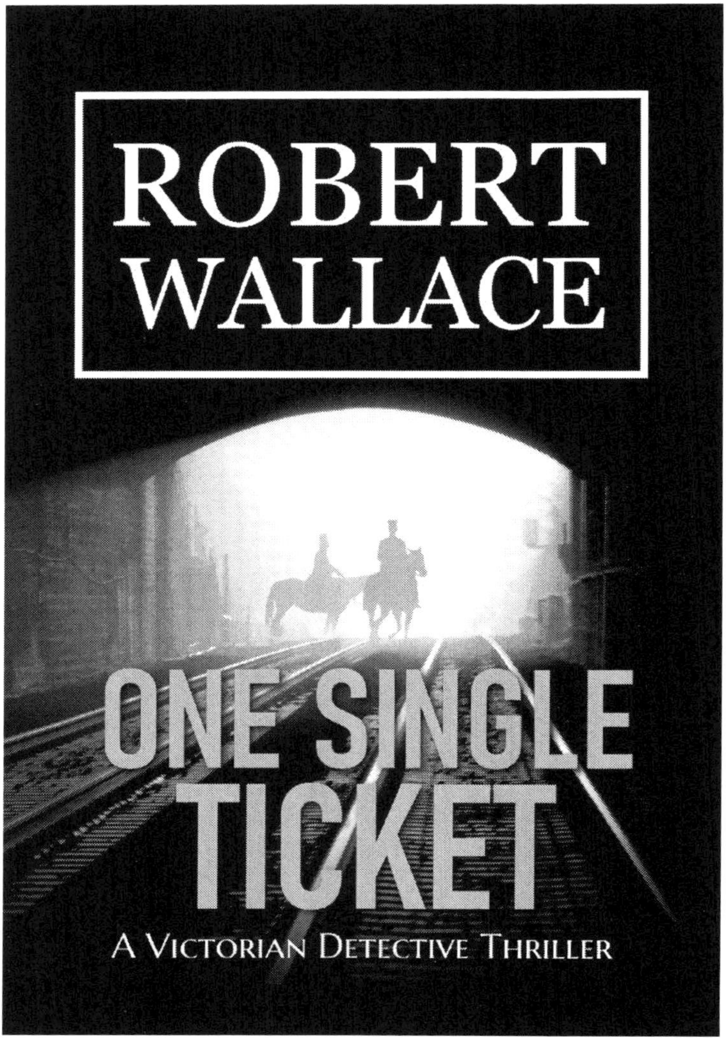
ROBERT
WALLACE
ONE SINGLE
TICKET
A VICTORIAN DETECTIVE THRILLER

XVII

Printed in Great Britain
by Amazon

54169270R00108